A MERRY MURDER AT ST. BERNARD CABINS

A WAGGING TAIL COZY MYSTERY

CINDY BELL

CONTENTS

CHAPTER 1

$\mathcal{N}$ikki Green tucked a folded sweater into her suitcase and smiled to herself as her fingertips coasted across the soft material. There weren't many occasions to wear it, as the weather near the bay was generally mild. There were some chillier days, but certainly no snow. The idea of being able to make snowmen, and get in a snowball fight thrilled her. The snowball fight would undoubtedly happen, since she would be spending time with her brother Kyle. Kyle was a couple of years younger than Nikki. He prioritized travel in his life, and in order to support his desire to wander, he took jobs along the way. His current gig had him stationed at *St. Bernard Cabins*, a high-end ski resort. Due to some under-booking over the holidays, the resort had a few empty cabins and asked the staff if they had any friends or family that would like to book them at a cut-rate price.

"It's good to be my sister, Nikki." Kyle laughed as he spoke to her on the phone earlier in the week. "The benefits are endless, aren't they?"

Both Nikki and her parents had decided to book a cabin. It had been quite some time since they all had Christmas together. She felt a buzz of excitement as she added the last few garments to her suitcase. She zipped it shut, then glanced around her room one last time to make sure she hadn't forgotten anything. She'd already arranged for another dog walker to cover her usual rounds, everything was in place.

The sound of her phone ringing jolted her out of the mental checklist she'd been running through. She checked the ID and saw that it was Mrs. Whitter calling.

"Hi Mrs. Whitter."

"Oh Nikki, it's a total disaster." She sighed.

"What is?" Nikki braced herself. Mrs. Whitter could be a bit overly dramatic about things. The disaster might be a leak in the kitchen, or it might be that her Chihuahua, Princess lost her favorite toy.

"I had everything arranged, absolutely everything, and would you believe now they tell me they don't allow dogs?" Mrs. Whitter huffed. "A tiny little pup isn't going to cause any harm to anything at all!"

"Wait, who doesn't allow dogs? I thought you were going to visit your niece?" Nikki frowned as she sat down on the edge of her bed. "Tell me everything from the beginning."

"Yes, I'm going to visit my niece. She is fine with Princess coming. But I hired a car service to drive me there, and I asked the woman on the phone specifically if they allowed pets, and she assured me that they do. Well, I called to confirm everything today, and surprise! No, they don't allow dogs. I even offered to pay an extra fee. I've called all the other services and they're all booked up. I can't drive my little car up there, besides if I'm driving no one can cuddle Princess and make sure she's safe and happy. I've promised to make my plum pudding for my niece and her family, and I won't be able to do it. I'll be stuck here for the holidays."

"Oh Mrs. Whitter, I'm so sorry. That must be so frustrating." Nikki felt terrible at the thought of Mrs. Whitter, who had become a good friend of hers, being alone for the holidays. "Where does your niece live again?"

"In Haggerty. It's too late to even book a flight, though I would hate to take Princess on a plane." Mrs. Whitter sniffed. "But no matter, there's no point in dwelling on things that can't be changed."

"Maybe it still can be." Nikki glanced at her watch. "Would you be able to leave in a few hours?"

"I had planned on leaving in the morning, but yes, everything is already packed up. Why?"

"I'm driving to Lowlar, it's not far from Haggerty, I can drop you and Princess off there on my way. What do you think?" Nikki smiled at the thought of being able to brighten her day.

"Are you sure about that, Nikki? I wouldn't want to put you out." Mrs. Whitter hesitated.

"I'm sure, in fact, I insist. I wasn't looking forward to driving all alone anyway. It will be great to have some company." Nikki stood up and began to go over her mental checklist again. "We'll leave around one, if that's okay with you?"

"That's perfect. I'll call my niece and let her know. Thank you so much, Nikki." Mrs. Whitter's tone brightened.

"I'm so happy I could help. I'll pick you up at one, Mrs. Whitter." As soon as Nikki hung up her phone, it began to ring again. She answered quickly and laughed. "Mrs. Whitter, I insist."

"I'm afraid this isn't Mrs. Whitter," a man replied.

"Jake!" Nikki laughed. "I'm sorry, I was just on the phone with another client and I thought she'd called back."

"That's all right. But I have a big problem." Jake cleared his throat.

"You do? Is Coco okay?" Nikki thought about the last time she'd walked Coco, a German Shepherd. He'd been fine when she'd dropped him off at home that morning.

"Yes, he's fine. But I have to work out of town for the holidays now, work just told me. Someone got sick and I have to cover them. I know it's very last minute, and you weren't going to work for the week, but I would be willing to pay extra if you would pet sit Coco." Jake groaned. "I'm really over a barrel here. All of the kennels are booked already, and there's no way I can take him with me. So, can you do it?"

"Oh wow, Jake, I'd love to. I really would. But I'm leaving town in a few hours. I'm so sorry. Is there anyone else you can leave him with?" Nikki began to run through possibilities of people she knew that might be able to take him, but they were all busy with the holidays.

"No, no one. Not going is really going to upset my boss. I just don't know what else to do. Thanks anyway, Nikki. Merry Christmas."

"You too, Jake." Nikki frowned as she started to hang up the phone. Then an idea popped into her mind. "Wait, Jake, are you still there?"

"Yes, what is it?" A twinge of hope lightened his voice.

"What if I take Coco with me? I'll be gone for just about a week, too, and if you're not back when I get back, I can always stay at your place until you are. I know it's a little odd, but it could work, couldn't it?" Nikki smiled at the thought. Coco was a great companion, and she was sure he would love the snow. Coco and Princess got along well with other dogs, and they had met each other before. Even though they hadn't spent much time together, Nikki knew that it wouldn't be a problem for them to travel together.

"I guess that could work. You wouldn't mind? I'm sure you have lots of plans."

"No, I wouldn't mind at all. I'll give you all of the information for the resort, and we'll video chat with you whenever you'd like so you can check on him. But if I'm going to take him, I'd have to pick him up soon. I really want to make it to the resort before it gets too dark." She began to reorganize her checklist in her mind. Adding a canine companion to her travels would require a few more things.

"Sure, oh Nikki you're a lifesaver. Thanks so much! I'm sure Coco will have a great time with you. I'll have him ready." Jake laughed. "You have no idea how relieved I am."

"No problem. I always look forward to spending time with Coco. I'll be there a little after twelve." Nikki hung up the phone and laughed to herself. Her quiet getaway had turned into a group excursion.

By twelve, Nikki was exhausted. Between phone calls, rearranging space in the SUV she rented for the trip, and adding a few last-minute items to her luggage, she'd been going nonstop since she'd hung up the phone with Jake. As she spread out blankets on the backseat of the SUV, she smiled to herself. Maybe it was a little chaotic, but she looked forward to the drive, and to having Coco as her companion for the week. Although, she didn't have enough space in her apartment to have a dog of her own, she often thought of the dogs she walked as her own, and that was especially true with Coco. She'd been walking him for a long time, and since his owner often traveled for business she would dog sit, or take him for special outings on the weekends now and then. It was an honor to her that Jake trusted her so much with his dog.

After one last check to make sure that she hadn't forgotten anything, Nikki climbed into the driver's seat of the SUV. The road that led to Coco's house ran right in front of the police department. Her heart skipped a beat as she passed it. Yes, she would love to spend the holidays with Quinn, but he had a very busy life. She resisted the urge to stop in and wish him a Merry Christmas. She'd already sent him a card, and left cookies at his door. If she did anything more, he'd either think she was obsessed with Christmas or obsessed with him. She stepped on the gas until she was a good distance from the police station. They had become good friends, and although Nikki hoped for something more, it hadn't progressed any further than friendship.

Nikki parked in the driveway of Coco's house and stepped out. After a quick glance at her watch she hoped that Jake would have Coco ready to go. By the time she got to Mrs. Whitter's and packed her things in the SUV, they would already be running a little behind schedule.

The front door swung open and Coco bounded out.

"Hi buddy." Nikki smiled as he jumped up to greet her.

"Coco, down! You know better." Jake huffed as he stepped out of the house.

"Don't worry, Jake. He's usually very well-mannered. He just knows I love his hugs." Nikki scratched the top of Coco's head as he dropped back down on to all four paws.

"I really appreciate you doing this. I put some things together for him." Jake handed her a small bag. "He's really good in the car, so I don't think the trip should be too bad."

"Great. I'll make sure he has plenty of chances to stretch his legs." Nikki pulled out a small card that she'd written all of the resort information on. "Here's where we'll be, and of course feel free to call or text anytime you'd like."

"Thanks." Jake met her eyes. "I mean it." He handed her an envelope. "I don't want to hear a word about the extra, there's some for taking him for the week, and a Christmas bonus. I want you to have a great vacation."

"Thanks Jake!" Nikki tucked the envelope into her purse. "I'll do my best not to argue."

"Good." Jake turned away as his cell phone rang. "Ugh, I've really got to run. Sorry Nikki."

"It's no problem. Coco and I are going to have a great time." Nikki opened the back door of the SUV and Coco jumped in.

CHAPTER 2

*A*fter the short drive to Mrs. Whitter's mansion, Nikki took a moment to check the weather. Despite the rather mild weather that surrounded her at the moment, she knew that just a few hours away winter was in full swing. As she checked the weather along the route to the resort, she was relieved to see that everything looked pretty clear. She might be able to make up some time along the way.

When Nikki walked up to the front door, Coco stuck his head out through the rear window and whimpered.

"Don't worry, buddy, I'll be right back." Nikki knocked lightly on the door.

CINDY BELL

"Come in, Nikki! Come in!" Mrs. Whitter's voice rang out from a distance.

Nikki tried the door, then pushed it open. Princess trotted up to her, took one sniff of her hand, then began to bounce back and forth in front of her.

"Oh, you smell Coco, don't you?" Nikki scooped the tiny dog up into her arms. "That's right, you're going to have a friend for the drive."

"I'll be right there, Nikki, I'm just grabbing a few last-minute things." Mrs. Whitter passed through the hallway and hurried towards her bedroom.

"No need to rush. Let me know if there's anything I can do to help." Nikki set Princess back down on the floor, and glanced around the large foyer. Mrs. Whitter's home was one of the finest in the neighborhood, not only because of its size, but because of its décor. She took special care to make sure everything was in just the right place and accentuated in just the right way. It was a skill Nikki hadn't acquired herself.

"All set." Mrs. Whitter walked out with a small suitcase in her hand.

"Let me take that. Is that all you're bringing?" Nikki took the suitcase from her hand.

"That's my suitcase. Princess' stuff is over there." Mrs. Whitter pointed to a pile of fluffy, pink bags.

"Oh wow!" Nikki laughed.

"It's not too much, is it? Will it fit?" Mrs. Whitter picked up Princess. "I just want to make sure that she has everything she needs. It'll be so strange for her to be away from home. I don't want her to be too nervous."

"I understand, and yes, there's plenty of room. I'll go ahead and load this up."

"Thank you. Princess likes the snow, but I need to make sure she is warm, especially if it snows."

"Of course." Nikki grabbed a few of the pink bags.

"I am also bringing this box of treats for my niece." Mrs. Whitter pointed to a box. "Is that okay?"

"Sure." Nikki nodded. She loaded up the SUV, then went back to get the last of the bags. "Are you ready to go?"

"Yes, we're all set. Thanks so much, again." Mrs. Whitter carried Princess out to the car.

"It's no problem at all. I'm looking forward to singing Christmas songs the whole way with you." Nikki finished loading the trunk.

"Oh well, that sounds lovely." Mrs. Whitter managed a smile.

"Don't worry, I'm just kidding." Nikki laughed. "I would never put you through that."

"Oh, thank goodness! I don't mind a little Christmas music, but I'm not much of a singer." Mrs. Whitter patted the top of Princess' head. "You like to bark along though don't you, Princess?"

"Princess can hop in the back if you'd like." Nikki opened the back door of the SUV and took Princess from Mrs. Whitter. "I've put some blankets down."

"Perfect. She does like to ride in my lap, but I think she'll be fine back there, too." Mrs. Whitter opened the passenger side door and climbed up onto the seat as Nikki placed Princess on the backseat. "My my, they make these monstrosities bigger every year, don't they? Soon I'll need a stepstool."

"Sorry about that, Mrs. Whitter. I wanted something bigger for the trip since it's a long drive, plus we might hit some snowy roads along the way." Nikki walked around to the driver's seat.

"Nikki, listen, if we're going to drive all this way together, I have one request." Mrs. Whitter turned to face her as she opened the driver's side door.

"What's that?" Nikki braced herself as she

hoped it wouldn't have anything to do with the radio.

"I think it's time you started calling me Sonia." Mrs. Whitter held Nikki's gaze. "We're friends aren't we, dear?"

"Of course, we are." Nikki smiled. "Sonia." It felt strange at first, but good as well.

As Sonia buckled her seat belt, she suddenly gasped.

Nikki looked over in time to see Coco stick his head between the front seats and lick Sonia's cheek.

"Oh my! What is Coco doing here?" Sonia gulped as she dodged another lick.

"Coco, no!" Nikki gasped and laughed at the same time. She grabbed the dog's collar and tugged him away from Sonia. "Didn't you get my last message?" Nikki gave Coco a few pets to calm him down, and the dog curled up on the backseat. Princess began to crawl all over him. "Princess looks pretty happy to see her friend." Nikki grinned.

"Oh no, I forgot to listen to it. Then I remembered when you pulled up the driveway and I just figured whatever it was you could tell me about it in person. Is Coco going on vacation with you?" Sonia fluffed her hair and shot a brief look at the dog over her shoulder. "He's not very well-mannered, is he?"

"He normally is. He's just a little excited." Nikki settled in the driver's seat again and buckled her seat belt. "Yes, it turns out that his owner has no one to watch him over the holidays, so I'm taking him with me to the cabins. It'll be nice to have him there."

"You're such a good person, Nikki." Sonia gave her a light pat on the back of her hand. "Always helping people."

"I don't mind." Nikki started the car. "I've had a lot of help from my wonderful friends." She winked at Sonia, then steered the car down her long driveway.

"Speaking of wonderful friends, what is Quinn doing for the holidays?"

"Not even out of the driveway yet and you're already asking about Quinn?" Nikki shot a sidelong look in her direction. "Are we going to talk about this for the whole drive?"

"I just asked a question." Sonia held up her hands with an innocent smile.

"Sure, sure." Nikki laughed and started towards the highway. "I did talk to him this morning. I think he was a little disappointed that I wouldn't be around for the holidays."

"Mmhm, I bet he was. All that eggnog and mistletoe." Sonia winked.

"Sonia!" Nikki laughed and shook her head. "We are just good friends. He said he'd be busy with a conference most of the week, anyway."

"You should have invited him." Sonia nodded. "Snow, fireplaces, all quite romantic."

"Enough." Nikki groaned and turned on the radio.

"Okay, okay, I'll stop." Sonia smiled as Princess climbed into the front seat to snuggle in her lap. "I just want to see you happy."

"Thanks Sonia." Nikki looked over at her with a warm smile. "I do appreciate that. And I am happy. I'm really glad we get to take this ride together."

"Me too." Sonia scratched Princess' tummy. "Drives like these remind me of my husband. He so loved to take trips. I so hated to." She laughed. "I would complain and complain, but he would convince me to go, and once we did, I always enjoyed myself. I have always liked an adventure."

"But you still fought him the next time?" Nikki glanced over at her.

"Sure. He loved a good argument. We were never mean to each other, we'd just bicker a bit, it always ended in a good laugh." Sonia grunted. "Oh, and once with a food fight."

"A food fight? Now that sounds like fun." Nikki flashed a smile at her. "It sounds like you two had a great relationship."

"Oh, it had its good moments, and its bad moments, just like all marriages. But yes, we loved each other." Sonia leaned closer to Nikki. "That's why I know it when I see it."

"Oh, not this again." Nikki turned up the radio just as a particularly loud rendition of *Rudolph the Red Nosed Reindeer* began to play.

After a few hours and numerous potty breaks, Nikki realized her plan to arrive by five wasn't going to happen. In fact, she hoped she'd make it by seven. As they neared Haggerty, she noticed that Sonia looked fairly sleepy.

"We'll be there soon." Nikki turned the radio down. "Sorry it took longer than expected."

"Well, no one knew there would be all this snow." Sonia gestured to the windshield as the snow continued to fall.

"It was supposed to be clear pretty much all the way." Nikki frowned and turned up the windshield wipers.

"It's all the new-fangled technology!" Sonia

waved her hand through the air. "The weather will always do its own thing."

"I guess you're right." Nikki took the exit off the highway for Haggerty.

After a few more minutes of driving, the GPS on her phone began making an unusual demand.

"Make a U-turn. Make a U-turn."

"What? Why?" Nikki sighed as she stared at the phone. "There's no reason for us to turn around."

"This is the way, I'm sure. I've made this drive before." Sonia peered through the windshield. "When you took care of Princess for me."

"This snow is not helping. I'm going to pull over." Nikki pulled to the side of the road and put the car in park. "Are you sure you gave me the right address?" She looked over the map on her phone.

"Yes, I'm certain. I wrote it down twice just to make sure." Sonia showed her the small slip of paper.

"It just seems odd that the GPS keeps telling me to turn around." Nikki gritted her teeth and tried not to be unnerved by the repetition of the GPS' demands.

"These new-fangled things, they'll send you right off a cliff if you let them." Sonia rolled her eyes.

"You are right about that." Nikki laughed. "We'll

just keep going, what's the worst that could happen?"

"Sounds good." Sonia began to gather her purse and other items around her feet. "We should be there in about fifteen minutes I'd say."

"Or not." Nikki slowed the SUV down, then brought it to a full stop. Her headlights shone through the steady snow enough to reveal a large, orange sign in the middle of the road.

"Road closed." Nikki frowned. "Sonia, we're not going to be able to get through."

"Let me give my niece a call. I'm sure this is some kind of mistake." Sonia pulled her phone out of her purse. "Just give me a second, Nikki, and we'll have all of this straightened out."

"Let's turn the heat up a bit." Nikki began to fiddle with the heating system which she hadn't quite figured out. As she did, she wondered if the roads to the ski resort would be blocked off as well. She grabbed her phone and checked the weather again. The surprise snowstorm had shocked most of the weather forecasters and didn't show any signs of letting up. She sent a text to her brother.

Stuck in some bad snow. I hope we'll be there soon.

Nikki sighed as she set the phone back down on her leg, then glanced over at Sonia. She held the phone tight to her ear and leaned forward as if she could get a bit closer to her niece by doing so.

"You guys okay back there?" Nikki looked into the back seat. She smiled at the sight of Coco and Princess snuggled close and sound asleep. At least they didn't seem to mind the snow.

"Nikki." Sonia winced as she hung up the phone. "I'm afraid I have some bad news."

CHAPTER 3

"*B*ad news?" Nikki looked over at Sonia with wide eyes.

"My niece said there's no way in or out of town. There's been a blizzard, and with the holidays it's going to take a few days to clear it all out." Sonia tried to smile.

"It's okay, Sonia." Nikki leaned across the front seat and hugged her. "You can come stay with me at the ski resort. If the roads get cleared up, I can always drive you back. What do you think?"

"Oh Nikki, I've already asked too much of you. You can just drop me off at the next hotel. Princess and I will be just fine." Sonia tucked her phone back into her purse. "I suppose this trip just wasn't meant to be."

"Absolutely not! I'd love to have you and Princess with me. Trust me, the cabin is going to be very nice and have plenty of room. Besides, my family would love to see you." Nikki backed the SUV away from the sign. "Don't worry, I'm sure by the morning we can figure all of this out." She looked over at Sonia. "Okay?"

"Well, if you insist." Sonia shrugged, then smiled. "I won't turn it down."

"Great." Nikki reset the directions for the cabin. "We should make a stop and stretch our legs, let the pups run a little." She glanced back at Coco and smiled as he snored. "Although, they don't seem to be complaining."

"No, but I am." Sonia winced and squirmed in her seat. "Sorry, I was trying to hold it until we got to Haggerty, but I really need a restroom."

"Don't worry, I'll stop at the next place I see." Nikki focused on her driving as the snowfall continued to increase. When she pulled off at a gas station, she could see that the snow had begun to pile up. A hint of fear bolted through her. What if they didn't make it to the cabin? Would she get stranded with Sonia and the two dogs? The thought left her unsettled.

While Sonia hurried into the shop to use the

restroom, Nikki put little boots on Princess' paws to protect them from the snow. Nikki did her best to coax the dogs out of the car. Neither dog seemed eager to get out in the snow. Once Coco jumped down, Nikki placed Princess on the ground. Seconds later they were both chasing each other and prancing through the snow. Nikki pulled her hood tighter around her face as a shiver carried along her spine.

When Sonia returned, Nikki herded the dogs inside the SUV.

"I'm just going to run in for a minute and grab a cup of coffee. Would you like one. or anything else?"

"No thanks."

"Okay, I'll be right back."

Nikki jogged towards the entrance of the shop as the snow started coming down harder. As she grabbed a coffee pot and poured herself a cup, she noticed a man beside her who seemed to be waiting for the same pot.

"Here you go." She smiled as she offered it to him. "Anything to keep warm right?"

"I don't mind the snow." He took the pot and poured a tall cup. "I've had a long drive."

"Me too. Merry Christmas." She smiled at him.

"Sure, thanks." He nodded. "You too."

As Nikki headed to the register, she heard him step up behind her. She paid for her coffee, then stepped aside. He piled a variety of things onto the counter. She thought it was a little odd to buy ice cream in the middle of a snowstorm, but it was another item that really caught her attention. Who bought sunglasses in the middle of a snowstorm?

"Good luck on your travels." Nikki did her best to meet his eyes.

"Thanks." He grunted, then suddenly looked up at her.

Nikki immediately noticed his dark green eyes. They seemed quite cold. He had short, spiky, black hair and appeared to be in his thirties.

"Ma'am, your change." The clerk behind the counter waved his hand in front of her.

"Oh, right. Thanks." Nikki took the change that she had completely forgotten about. She glanced once more at the man who continued to stare at her, then turned and hurried out the door and straight to the SUV.

"All set?" Sonia smiled at Nikki as she climbed into the SUV.

"Sure." Nikki started the engine, then looked back towards the gas station once more. The snow fell too hard for her to see much of anything. Once they were on the road again it was a slow crawl towards the resort. The time crept by, and the snow on the ground kept rising. When she finally turned into the driveway that led to the cabins, she was relieved. She parked in front of the main lobby and looked over at Sonia who had fallen asleep in the passenger seat. She gave her shoulder a gentle shake.

"Sonia, we're here."

"Hmm?" Sonia's eyes fluttered open. "Oh. Okay. I'll get my things." She started to gather up her purse.

"Just wait here, I need to check in, then we'll drive to the cabin. Okay?" Nikki stepped out of the SUV. "Turn the heat up if you need to."

As Nikki walked into the lobby her eyes widened. A massive fireplace stood on one wall, the opposite wall was made up of floor to ceiling windows which gave a stunning view of the snow as it continued to fall. There were several overstuffed couches and chairs scattered throughout the large space. In one corner a sprawling café space promised to be a wonderful place for a snack when it opened up again in the morning.

The crackling of the fire, combined with the soft

music that played through hidden speakers around the lobby made Nikki aware of just how exhausted she was from the journey. A red-haired woman stood behind a large desk with her back to Nikki. She appeared to be sorting through some paperwork. Nikki walked up to the front counter and tugged her wallet out of her purse. She waited a minute to see if the woman would notice her. When she didn't, Nikki leaned forward some.

"Excuse me? I'd like to check in."

A burst of laughter drew Nikki's attention to a group of people near the door of the lobby. She noticed that four of the men appeared to be about her age, while the fifth looked to be in his forties. He chuckled as he shook his head at the younger men.

"Just wait until you get to be my age, you'll see that you should have had a lot more fun in your younger years."

Nikki looked back at the woman just as she turned around to face her. Though she had delicate features, and a flawless complexion, she struck her as harsh. Perhaps, it was because of her tense lips and her knitted eyebrows. She studied Nikki as if there was something about her that she instantly did not approve of. She flipped open a large book on the desk between them.

"Welcome to *St. Bernard Cabins*."

"Thank you."

"Sign in. Right here." She jabbed a long, blood-red fingernail towards an empty space on the page. "Don't skip a line, I hate it when people skip a line."

"I won't." Nikki was shocked, this woman was rude. Where was the customer service?

"You're late for check-in." The woman eyed her from behind thick, blue glasses. "You were supposed to be here by five."

"I know, I'm sorry. We ran into some bad weather on the way." Nikki scribbled her name in the book. "I know that you accept pets. I have some unexpected company."

"Oh, we're very pet friendly. Not to worry." She smiled. "What kind of cat do you have?"

"No cats, just two dogs." Nikki smiled in return.

"Oh, dogs." The woman's smile faded. "Sure, we take those, too. We'll just need an additional pet deposit."

"No problem." Nikki peered past the woman at a shelf full of framed pictures of cats. "Are those your cats?"

"My babies, yes." She beamed. "Itsy, Bitsy, Boo, and Hilda."

"Aw, what cute names. They're beautiful." Nikki

set the pen back down in the book. "Are you the manager here?"

"No, I'm the owner. Well, co-owner." She jabbed her finger in the direction of a tall, slender man who stood near a group of guests beside the front door. "Max and Gloria Merner, we just recently bought the place."

"Oh, I see, well it's beautiful. I'm looking forward to my stay here." Nikki tipped her head towards the small café. "Is there breakfast in the morning?"

"Oh yes, everything is listed here." Gloria slid a pamphlet across the counter to her. "And here are your room keys." She set two cards on top of the pamphlet. "If you have any issues with the room you can press the red button on your phone, it will connect you with Ashley, our housekeeper."

"Wonderful, thanks so much. Merry Christmas." Nikki gathered up the pamphlet and cards.

"Merry Christmas to you, too." She gave Nikki a short wave, then walked off to join her husband. Nikki noticed that she seemed to relax when she spoke about her cats and became a lot nicer.

Nikki hurried back to the SUV and popped open the driver's side door.

"I've got everything we need." She flashed a

smile to Sonia and the two dogs in the back. "The cabin is just down the hill." As she navigated her way through the snow to the cabin, she was relieved not to have to drive much farther in the snow. "Let me unlock the door so you three can get inside and get warm. Then I'll get the bags."

"Don't be silly, I can unlock the door." Sonia winked at her, then took a room card.

Nikki parked in front of the cabin, then opened the driver's side door to step out. Before she could get her foot down, someone grabbed her by the arm and tugged her out of her seat.

"Nikki!"

Her scream was cut short by laughter as she recognized her brother's face as he pulled her into a warm hug. Nikki was very petite, and she felt even smaller next to her tall brother. His hugs always engulfed her and made her feel safe.

"Finally!" Kyle laughed as he slapped her shoulder. "Weren't you supposed to be here hours ago?"

"Weren't you supposed to warn me about snow-storms?" Nikki raised an eyebrow.

"Oh right." Kyle grinned. "That one came out of nowhere. I'm glad you got here safe, sis." He patted her on the shoulder. "And it looks like you have company?" His eyes shone as he looked past her into the SUV. "Is that Mrs. Whitter?"

"It sure is, and her dog, Princess. I also brought a dog friend of my own. Coco, meet Kyle." Nikki held the back door open so that Coco could jump out.

"Oh, isn't he a beauty!" Kyle grinned as he crouched down to greet the dog. "Did Gloria take care of you okay?"

"Yes, she's a bit grumpy, but everything's fine. I just needed to put down an additional pet deposit. I'll fill you in on everything. I need to grab the bags. Do you want to help Sonia to the door?" Nikki glanced over her shoulder just in time to see Sonia by the front door. "Okay, never mind." She laughed.

"She's as spry as ever. Let me help you with the bags." Kyle opened the trunk.

"Thanks."

"Wow, that's a lot of pink bags."

"They are Princess'." Nikki smiled as she grabbed a few of the bags and let Kyle take the rest.

"I should have guessed." Kyle chuckled.

"You're not supposed to be here!" A sharp, female voice carried out of the cabin as Sonia walked towards it.

CHAPTER 4

"**I** have the key, so that means I am supposed to be here!" Sonia shot back at the woman in the cabin. She placed her hands on her hips as Princess ran in circles around her feet.

"What's going on here?" Nikki looked past Sonia at a woman who towered at least a foot above her. "Who are you?"

"I'm Ashley, and the two of you must be in the wrong cabin. This cabin is supposed to be empty." Ashley narrowed her blue eyes and studied both of them. "Did Gloria mess this up? I bet she did. That woman can never get things straight."

"Listen, this is the keycard she gave us." Nikki took a deep breath to calm herself down. Her instinct was to protect Sonia, but she knew it was

33

always better to try to settle things instead of making them worse. "If we're in the wrong cabin, we'll gladly move. But maybe the confusion is because we checked in late?"

"I've got the rest of the bags, Nikki." Kyle dropped them just inside the door.

"You!" Ashley glowered in his direction. "I should have known you would have something to do with this."

"Ashley, so good to see you again." Kyle flashed her a charming smile. "Why are you harassing innocent people today?"

"Watch it!" Ashley snapped. "If you checked in late, then I wasn't notified at all, Gloria should have texted me." She slid a phone from the front pocket of her apron and glanced over it. Her lips pursed, then she tucked it back into her pocket. "Well, the cabin is as clean as it's going to get." She pushed past the three of them and headed out the door.

"Apparently, she was notified after all." Sonia rolled her eyes. "All of that bluster for nothing."

"That woman is nothing but bluster." Kyle shook his head. "Can you believe she doesn't like me?" His eyes widened. "Everyone likes me!"

"Of course, they do." Sonia gave him a few light

pats on the cheek. "It's those chubby cheeks of yours."

"Hey." Kyle laughed as he ducked away from her touch.

"She's right." Nikki grinned. "What's her problem with you, Kyle?" She led the two dogs into the kitchen and set down bowls of water for both of them.

"A couple of things. She asked me out when I first started working here. I turned her down. I was nice about it and everything, I just don't want any commitments. Ever since then she's had it in for me. Also I stay here, and I work at the ski lift up the hill. There's a ski lift that we're supposed to take to get up there. But it's always backed up, and it's so much quicker for me to just cut through the courtyard and walk up the hill. It drives her crazy apparently because I'm not supposed to do it." Kyle threw his hands in the air. "It's not like I go out of my way to walk in areas where people would be skiing. I make sure that I'm on an out-of-the-way path. But every single time I do it, she manages to spot me, and she starts throwing a fit."

"Well, if the rules are that you should take the ski lift, then maybe she has a point." Nikki raised an eyebrow as she gazed at her brother.

"No, she doesn't have a point. All of the guys do it. She only picks on me." Kyle slid his hands into his pockets. "Besides, don't start with me on the rule thing, Nikki. I know what I'm doing."

"I'm not trying to start anything." Nikki rubbed her hand across her forehead. "I'm honestly just tired. I really want to get the dogs settled and get to bed."

"I understand. If you need anything just text me. The snow is supposed to continue throughout the night, so we might end up snowed in by tomorrow. Can we meet for coffee in the morning?" Kyle lifted Sonia's suitcase onto her bed for her.

"Yes, sure we can do that. In the little café?" Nikki stretched her arms above her head and yawned.

"Yes. Usually Max has some delicious coffee going by about six. If you need to sleep later that's fine, though. I don't have to be in until eleven tomorrow." Kyle nodded to Sonia. "Good night, I hope you both get some good rest."

"Me too." Sonia covered her mouth as she yawned.

"Oh, I brought you some things. Be right back." Kyle ducked back out into the snow, seconds later he returned with a large garbage bag.

"What's that?" Nikki eyed the bag.

"Sorry, I didn't want everything to get snowy." Kyle opened up the bag and pulled out a heavy, thick coat. "I figured you probably wouldn't have anything too warm. You're going to need this. There are a few pairs of gloves, thick socks, a hat, and some scarves in there, too."

"Wow, thanks Kyle." Nikki looked up at her brother with surprise. "That's very thoughtful of you."

"Mom texted me." Kyle grinned. "She sent me a list of things to pick up."

"Of course, she did." Nikki laughed. "Are they in their cabin?"

"Oh, you didn't get their text?" He frowned. "This storm is causing the networks to glitch. Their flight got canceled. They're hoping to be able to leave tomorrow, but won't know until this storm settles down."

"Oh, that's terrible." Nikki sighed. "I hope they can get a flight out soon."

"Me too. Let me know if you guys need anything." Kyle waved to Sonia, then stepped through the door.

After Kyle left, Nikki began to unpack a few things she needed for herself, and for Coco.

"You weren't kidding, Nikki, this place is amazing." Sonia unzipped her suitcase. "I'm sure it will be absolutely stunning in the morning with all of the fresh snow."

"Yes, I bet it will be." Nikki smiled at the thought.

"I'm just going to unpack Princess' things quickly. Is it okay if I use this closet?" Sonia pointed to one of the closets.

"Sure." Nikki smiled as Sonia began to unpack Princess' stuff. "After a good night's sleep, I'm sure everything will seem a lot brighter. I'm going to change into my pajamas and sprawl out."

Coco jumped up on the bed and did just that.

"Oh nope, I don't think so, buddy. I brought your bed." Nikki grinned as she tossed down his large dog bed on the floor beside the bed.

Coco lifted his head, sniffed the air, then launched off the edge and landed in his bed.

"Good boy." Nikki walked over to give him a quick pet, then grabbed her pajamas from her suitcase. As she walked towards the bathroom, a knock on the door of the cabin made her pause.

"Kyle must have forgotten to tell me something." Nikki walked back to the door and pulled it open.

Instead of Kyle, she found a woman she didn't know.

"Hi, hi!" She smiled and shivered at the same time. "So cold out here. Mind if I come in?"

"Uh sure." Nikki took a step back so that the woman could get inside.

"I'm Betsy." She thrust her hand towards Nikki. It was hidden inside of a thick, florescent pink glove. "Oops sorry." She laughed and tugged the glove off, then extended her hand again.

"Nikki." She shook her hand, still uncertain of the woman's purpose for knocking on the door.

"I'm your cabin neighbor." Betsy gestured to the far wall of the cabin. "Just thought I'd pop over and introduce myself. I'm vacationing on my own, and I'm hoping to meet some new people." She looked past Nikki and waved at Sonia. "Oh, and you have dogs. How wonderful!" She made a strange squeaking sound in her throat. "They're tame, right?"

"Yes." Nikki smiled as she noticed that Coco hadn't even budged from his bed.

"Princess wouldn't hurt a fly." Sonia picked her up and walked towards Nikki and Betsy. "I'm Sonia Whitter. Did you really come out in a snowstorm to say hello?"

"Yes, I did. I know, it's a bit silly, but I'm just the friendly sort." Betsy adjusted the colorful scarf around her neck. "But it's just so cold out there."

"You should think about getting a thicker scarf." Sonia eyed it dubiously. "It won't do much for keeping you warm with all of those holes in it."

"It's okay, I like it. I made it actually." Betsy tugged on one end of the scarf. "It's one of the many things I make. *Betsy's Crafts*, that's the name of my online shop." She reached into her pocket and pulled out two business cards. "Here. Just in case you're ever in the market for something unique and handmade."

"Thanks." Nikki smiled as she took the card. "I'll keep you in mind."

"Have a good night, you two. I'm sure we'll see each other again." She waved to both of them, then stepped back out through the door.

Nikki closed it and looked over at Sonia.

"Perky, isn't she?" Sonia grinned.

"I'm sure I'll be more friendly in the morning." Nikki laughed.

After Nikki and Sonia changed, they both settled into bed. A few hours into a heavy slumber, the sound of a whimper woke Nikki up. Uncertain of what it could be, she felt uneasy for a few seconds, until she remembered that she had two canine companions.

"Oh seriously?" Nikki rolled over in her bed and looked at Princess who stood near the cabin door. She whined again.

Nikki didn't want her to wake Sonia. She sighed and pushed her blanket off. On her way to the door she grabbed the heavy coat Kyle had left her, and shoved her arms through it. She slid her feet into her boots and snapped Princess' leash onto her collar.

"Okay buddy, let's take care of this."

Nikki opened the door and winced at the blast of icy air that struck her in the face. It was so cold that it stung. She ducked her head against the still falling snow, then stepped out into it. Princess began to sniff around the snow.

Nikki's teeth began to chatter. She thought about hot coffee, and hot cocoa, and hot apple pie. She thought about how warm and cozy her bed would be when she crawled back into it.

"Let's go, Princess, do your thing." Nikki sighed as she waited for Princess.

Nikki gave Princess a little slack on the leash so that she could explore and hopefully do her business. As she kicked up a bit of snow behind her,

CINDY BELL

Nikki pictured a tropical beach. She was lost in the smell of the sea, when Princess started digging in the snow.

"Okay, that's enough." Princess dug faster. "What are you getting into, Princess?" She frowned as she walked up behind her. Princess was usually a dainty dog, something must have got her attention. As Nikki watched, Princess dug a scarf free from the snow. It was colorful, and too thin to do much good in the cold weather. Nikki guessed that someone had dropped it on their way back to their cabin.

"All right, let me have it, Princess." Nikki reached for it. As she did, she took a step forward. She stepped on something soft. She looked down. "Oh no!" She gasped and stumbled back a few steps. Her right foot slid in the snow and she tumbled backwards. When she hit the ground, cushioned by several inches of snow, the impact jolted her back to her senses. "Help!" She cried out, suddenly very aware that she'd left her cell phone inside the cabin. "Help! Someone help!"

"Nikki?" Sonia paused at the door of the cabin. "What is it? What's wrong? Is Princess okay?"

"Call 9-1-1, Sonia, someone is out here in the

snow!" Nikki bit into her bottom lip as she stared at the body half-covered in snow. "It's Ashley!"

As Nikki spun back around towards the body in the snow, the scarf still clutched in her hand, she noticed a pile of broken, black plastic not far from a large boot print in the snow. The state of Ashley's hair and clothes made her believe that she hadn't died of natural causes. Her hair was in a mess around her face. Her right foot was missing a boot. Nikki swept her gaze across the snow, and saw it not far off. Had she been running? Had it slipped off when she tried to get away from someone? Nikki's stomach churned at the thought. Cabin doors began to open, hushed voices spoke to one another, but no one approached Nikki or the body. Nikki shivered as a cold breeze swirled snow around her face. Despite knowing that Ashley was no longer alive, she couldn't bring herself to leave her alone in the cold.

CHAPTER 5

Strange sirens brought Nikki back to reality as the dark evening lit up with flashing lights. She watched as two snowmobiles buzzed into the area. They stopped a good distance away, and the two riders began to approach. Nikki noticed one officer was a man, about six-foot tall, and the other was a woman about six inches shorter than him. As they walked towards Nikki, she could make out their uniforms. She felt some relief that the police had arrived. Certainly, they would know what to do next.

"What happened here?" the woman asked as she looked over Ashley's body.

"I don't know. I brought my dog out, well she's

not my dog, but I'm traveling with her owner, to use the bathroom, and we found her. Her name is Ashley." Nikki held Princess tightly in her arms.

"Was Ashley," the man corrected.

"Was Ashley," Nikki repeated, a little stunned that he would make such a comment.

"Perhaps she had a heart attack." The woman pursed her lips as she looked over the body.

"No, I don't think so." Nikki held out the scarf she'd picked up. "Princess found this first. I'm sorry that I touched it, but I think it might have something to do with what happened here. Also, I noticed that Ashley's boot is back there some distance." She pointed towards it. "I think she must have been running."

"Oh right, good point." The woman nodded.

"What do you think, Schwitz? Maybe she was out for a jog?" The man shrugged. "This cold weather can wreak havoc on the body."

"No, I doubt that. At night? I don't think so. Maybe she was a little drunk? Conner get down there and take a sniff." Schwitz pointed towards Ashley.

"What? No." Conner held up his hands and took a step back. "I'm not sniffing anything."

"Ugh. Straighten up, Conner. We are the police,

remember? We have to figure out how this woman died?" Schwitz glowered at him.

"Are there other officers coming?" Nikki stared between the two, shocked at their banter.

"Just us, I'm afraid." Schwitz smiled. "All the roads are snowed in, and we're the only ones that patrol this area. Normally, we'd call some detectives in, but there's no way for them to get here in this." She gestured to the snow that still fell, though at a slower pace.

"Oh." Nikki's stomach twisted. She took a breath to help herself calm down. "Listen, I think Ashley struggled with someone. I don't think this is a death from accidental or natural causes. I think she's been murdered."

"Murdered?" Conner gasped and took another step back. "No way!"

"Conner, pull yourself together." Schwitz jabbed him in the side. "It just may be a murder. I'll be needing that." Schwitz snatched the scarf out of Nikki's hands. "And get this dog out of here before she contaminates the crime scene."

Nikki pulled Princess close. She stared at the two for a moment longer, then carried the dog back towards the cabin.

"Nikki, are you okay?" Sonia opened the door,

Coco was behind her. Sonia reached for Princess and held her in her arms. "Poor baby, I thought you both might freeze out there."

As Nikki filled her in on what she found, Sonia's concern turned to horror.

"You're sure it's Ashley, that awful woman from earlier?"

"Yes, it was her." Nikki bit into her bottom lip. "And Sonia, I'm pretty sure she was killed."

"Oh no! How?" Sonia's eyes widened as she patted Princess.

"My guess is she was strangled, but I don't know for sure. Maybe with the scarf that Princess found." Nikki shuddered. "It was so colorful, and crocheted. I don't know if it really would have been strong enough."

"I remember that awful scarf." Sonia scrunched up her nose. "The neighbor that stopped by earlier was wearing it. It clashed so badly with that pea green coat she had on."

"Oh yes, I remember it now. But I didn't look at it that closely. Maybe it's not the same one." Nikki looked up at her.

"It certainly sounds like the same one." Sonia stroked Princess' fur. "Do you think she had some kind of problem with Ashley?"

"I'm not sure what to think, yet." Nikki ran her hand across her forehead and closed her eyes. "I still can't believe what I saw."

"Nikki, you need to sit down." Sonia guided her to the table, and sat down across from her with Princess still held tightly in her arms.

"Nikki!" Kyle's voice called out from beyond the cabin door.

"In here, Kyle." Nikki stood up from the table and turned to face him as he stepped inside. A wave of dizziness threatened to knock her right back down. She took a breath, then forced a small smile. "Don't worry we're all okay."

"I was worried." Kyle walked up to her. "Why didn't you call me? Or text me? The sirens woke me up. When I saw the flashing lights over here, I thought the worst."

"I'm sorry, Kyle, I just thought it would be best to let you sleep. There's nothing you can do." Nikki sank back down into her chair. "Ashley's already gone."

"Nikki." Kyle rested his hand on her shoulder and looked down into her eyes. "Are you sure you're okay?"

"It was quite a shock." Sonia reached across the table and took Nikki's hand.

"How did you even find her?" Kyle glanced between the two of them.

"Princess needed a potty break. I took her outside, and she started digging. She found a scarf." Nikki paused and took a breath. "When I tried to get it from her, I stepped on something." She winced. "Then I looked down and saw it was Ashley." She wiped at her eyes as tears threatened to fall. "That poor woman. Who would do this to her?"

"Honestly, she wasn't well liked." Kyle winced. "I know that sounds cold of me to say, but it's the truth. Even Gloria and Max couldn't stand her. She was one of the few employees they kept on after they bought the place. And me specifically, she seemed to target. Like I said, I declined the offer to go out with her, but I'm not sure if that was the reason why."

"She wasn't too pleasant to us earlier today." Sonia blinked as she glanced at the clock on the wall. "Well, I guess that would have actually been yesterday. It's two in the morning."

"It is?" Nikki felt a rush of dizziness again. She had no idea what time it was when she took Princess out. "We should all get some sleep."

"Nikki, I'm sorry about all of this." Kyle hugged her. "Do you want me to stay here with you tonight?"

"No, you don't have to, but you can if you want. I'll sleep on the couch." Nikki wiped a hand across her face in an attempt to focus her mind on the moment at hand. Yet her thoughts shifted right back to the moment she found Ashley.

"No, it's fine. I'll take the couch." Kyle met her eyes. "Get some rest, Nikki. Hopefully all of this will be sorted out by the morning."

Nikki nodded as she crawled into her bed. Moments later the lights were out, and everything was quiet, but for Coco's snoring. She closed her eyes as her stomach twisted into knots. Somehow, she doubted that the sun coming up would fix anything.

Nikki woke up the next morning to the sound of the cabin door closing. She sat up in her bed and looked straight at Kyle.

"What are you doing? What time is it?" Nikki's gaze swung wildly in search of the clock.

"It's just after seven. I just spoke with the police officers." Kyle shoved his hands into his pockets.

"Oh?" Nikki wiped her eyes as reality began to set in around her. "Do they know who did it?"

"They think it was me." Kyle's eyes widened as he stared at Nikki. "The boot print is the same size as mine. I guess, Gloria and Max told them about the problems Ashley and I had."

"That's crazy. Why would you kill her over a little dispute?" Nikki jumped up from the edge of her bed. "Do you know these officers? Are they any good at their job?"

"Honestly, the worst crime I've seen since I've been here is someone stealing skis that belonged to someone else. But that turned out to be a misunderstanding, the skis had just gotten mixed up." Kyle ran his hand back through his hair. "Nikki, this whole thing is crazy. I can't believe that they're even considering me a suspect."

"Try not to worry." Nikki wrapped her arm around his shoulders. "It's still very early in the investigation, so I'm sure they're exploring every possibility. They'll check you off the suspect list in no time."

"I sure hope so." Kyle shifted from one foot to the other. "Not that it will matter. I'll probably still lose my job over it."

"Don't say that." Nikki pulled him closer and gave him a full hug. "Things will work out."

"Listen to me, worrying about my job." Kyle shook his head as he pulled away. "There's no reason for that, when someone has been killed. I'm going to see if there's anything I can do to help. Oh, and Gloria and Max have asked you to join them for coffee this morning."

"Just me?" Nikki glanced towards Sonia's bed and noticed that she still slept soundly.

"Yes, I think they want to talk to you about what happened. I can go with you if you want." He smiled. "You don't have to go at all if you don't want to."

"It's okay. I'd like to speak to them. I'm just going to take a shower first. Kyle, make sure you tell me before you speak to the police again. I have a friend I can call, a detective." Nikki met her brother's eyes. "You have to be careful what you say to them."

"Like you said, there's nothing to worry about. I didn't do it, so how could there be?" He shrugged, then left the cabin.

Nikki hurried to take a shower, then made sure her hair was dry. She could still remember the icy blast of the wind against her cheeks. A glance out the window revealed that the snow had finally stopped. She felt some relief but wondered if it even mattered anymore. Would her parents still want to come after what happened?

CHAPTER 6

*N*ikki left a note for Sonia, filled up the dogs' water and fed them. Sonia had already unpacked all of Princess' gourmet meals that she had prepared for her. They were in the small refrigerator and were organized by the time they should be given. There were little notes on each of the piles, so Nikki knew exactly what to give her. However, Nikki didn't need the notes. She knew Princess' menu from when she would pet sit her. Sonia had reminded Nikki on numerous occasions that Princess must have the chicken meal for dinner. She claimed that it helped Princess sleep. The beef meal was for breakfast to give her energy.

After feeding the dogs she trotted them outside to use the bathroom. She didn't want to risk one of them waking Sonia up. After the night they had, she wanted to make sure Sonia got all the sleep she needed. Nikki didn't take them out for long as she didn't want Princess to get too cold.

When Nikki let the dogs back into the cabin, she saw that Sonia was still asleep. She locked the door, and headed across the fresh snow to the lobby. The bright sun did nothing to ease the cold temperature. She shivered as she stepped through the door of the lobby and right into the middle of a conversation between two men who wore shirts with the resort's emblem on them.

"The last time was the worst, though." The older man frowned. "I thought I was going to have to step in."

"Why? Was Gloria going to deck her?" The younger man laughed.

"Keep quiet!" The older man gave him a hard shove. "This is serious. What if they did something to her?"

"Those two?" The younger man shook his head in disbelief. "No way. They're harmless. If anything, they should have been scared of Ashley. She was fierce. I never wanted to get on her bad side."

"Excuse me." Nikki smiled at the men as she attempted to step past.

"Oh, it's you isn't it?" The younger man stared at her. "I'm Dex, I saw you outside when Ashley's body was found. You're the one that found it, aren't you?"

"Yes, well technically I sort of fell over it." Nikki sighed as she realized she didn't want to explain the entire situation. "You two knew Ashley well?"

"We worked with her." Dex shrugged. "Gary and I didn't really spend any time with her, though."

"I didn't know her either. I only met her for a few minutes." Nikki looked past them, towards the café, which was empty, but for Max. He sat at a small table, while Gloria helped someone at the front desk. "She didn't get along with the owners?"

"That's an understatement." Gary rolled his eyes. "The three of them fought like cats and dogs."

"About what?" Nikki glanced between them. "They hadn't known each other long, had they?"

"Ashley had a special contract with the previous owners, so she got to stay on for a year after Max and Gloria purchased the place. She wanted to continue to do everything the way she was used to. Max and Gloria are all about changing and improving things."

"Interesting, that must have been quite a clash." Nikki glanced in the direction of Max again.

"Hey, you two! We're not paying you to talk to the guests!" Gloria waved her hand at the two men.

Nikki managed a smile as she stepped away from them and towards the café. Gloria nodded to her, then turned back to the guest at the front desk.

Nikki reached the table where Max sat and paused beside him.

"Hi." She stood awkwardly near the table.

"Nikki!" He jumped up from his chair and thrust his hand towards her. "The police have told me all about what you went through, I'm so sorry."

"It's all right." Nikki took his hand in a mild shake. "I'm just sorry that it happened at all."

"As am I." Max gestured to the chair across from him. "Please, sit, I'll bring you some coffee."

"Thanks." She eased herself down into the chair and watched as he hurried off to the coffee bar. A glance in the direction of the front desk revealed that Gloria had finished with the guest.

"Here you go." Max returned with a full cup. "It's the least we can do." He set a cup of coffee down in front of Nikki. "How are your dogs settling in?"

"Oh, they're fine." Nikki smiled. "Thanks for asking. I saw the pictures of your beautiful cats."

"Oh, did you?" Max nodded. "Well, they're

more Gloria's cats. I have two St. Bernards. Actually, originally we stayed here because of the name. I just love St. Bernards. As soon as I looked at it, I fell in love with the place. When it came up for sale at the perfect time, I just had to buy it." He pulled out his cell phone and showed her the picture on the display. "See? Fluffy and Marshmallow. Fluffy is still a puppy."

"How lovely." Nikki nodded and smiled. "I'd love to meet them sometime."

"I appreciate you coming in to speak to us." Max snapped his fingers in Gloria's direction, then pointed to the table.

"It's no problem." Nikki took a sip of her coffee.

Gloria walked over to the table with a wide smile plastered on her lips.

"Nikki, so good to see you." She took the third seat at the table.

"I do hope that you'll consider keeping what happened to yourself." Max sat back down across from Nikki. "I know that in this age of social media, and constant contact, it's tempting to spread a shocking story around, but it will cause so much damage to the resort."

"You don't have to worry, Max. I wouldn't share something like this." Nikki sat back in her chair and took another sip of coffee. "This is delicious."

"I brewed it myself." Max glanced over at Gloria, then looked back at Nikki. "The thing is, we haven't owned the resort long."

"I said, I understand." Nikki looked up at him. "My concern is more for Ashley's privacy, though. Doesn't she have family? Have they been notified?"

"Family? That beast?" Gloria rolled her eyes.

Nikki nearly choked on the hot coffee in her mouth. She swallowed hard, then cleared her throat.

"Beast?"

"Yes." Gloria shrugged. "I'm sorry, but I'm an honest person. I can't pretend to grieve for a woman who was only out for her own best interest. She would have done anything to swindle this resort out of our hands."

"Gloria, please." Max frowned at her. "We've talked about this. No matter what Ashley was like, she still didn't deserve to be strangled."

"Strangled?" Nikki looked between both of them. "Did the police confirm that?"

"Yes." Max nodded and sighed. "They were able to figure that much out."

"Those idiots will never solve this case." Gloria stood up abruptly from the table. "Just don't say a word about it, Nikki. Don't think that we don't know that your brother is the main suspect. If you decide to run your mouth about all of this, we can share a few things we know about him, too." She raised an eyebrow as she looked straight into Nikki's eyes.

"How dare you!" Nikki stood up so fast that her chair almost tipped over.

"Wait, she didn't mean that." Max stood up as well. "Gloria!"

"Don't you ever threaten my brother." Nikki glared back at her as her protective instincts kicked into gear. "He is completely innocent, and I will make sure that everyone knows it."

"We'll see about that." Gloria turned on her heel and stormed off.

"I'm sorry, I'm so sorry." Max held up his hands. "She gets a little wound up. She really didn't mean anything she just said. Please, don't worry about it."

"And just who am I supposed to believe?" Nikki turned her attention to him. "You, or your wife?"

"She won't do anything to Kyle. He's a good, young man, I know that. She knows that, too." Max stumbled over his words.

"She'd better not." Nikki stalked out of the lobby. Anger boiled in her chest as she made her way towards the cabin. If the roads weren't closed, she'd take Sonia, and Kyle, and leave. Unfortunately, she had no choice but to stay. As she neared the cabin, she was startled to see Sonia outside, with Princess, and a man who had his back to Nikki.

"Nikki, there you are." Sonia waved to her. "I was worried."

"Didn't you get my note?" Nikki paused in front of her.

"No, sorry I must have overlooked it. Have you met Ken?" Sonia gestured to the man beside her. "He's staying in the cabin across from ours. He came over to check on us, isn't that sweet?"

"Hi there." Ken turned towards her and offered his hand. Nikki was startled by the sight of his deep blue eyes. They added another dimension of beauty to his already handsome face. His short, light brown hair stuck out of the corner of his baseball cap. He appeared to be in his fifties, maybe a bit older, though his youthful face made her question that estimate.

"Hi." Nikki smiled as she shook his hand. "Thanks for your concern."

"Yes, after what happened last night, I just wanted to be sure that you were both okay." Ken adjusted the cap on his head. "I know it's not easy being in an unfamiliar place and having such a tragedy occur."

"No, it isn't." Nikki briefly considered what Quinn would have to say about all of this. Maybe he could help her sort it all out. But she knew he was very busy.

"I'll leave you two alone. I need to buy some ski goggles at the shop in the lobby before I go out skiing today." Ken nodded to each of them. "It was a pleasure to meet you both."

"You as well, Ken. Come by anytime to share some tea." Sonia winked at him, then led Princess back into the cabin. Nikki followed behind her.

"He seems nice." Nikki crouched down to greet Coco and scratched behind his ears. "Hi buddy."

"He does. Isn't he handsome?" Sonia wiggled her eyebrows. "I don't mind him calling on me anytime."

"Sonia, you have a crush?" Nikki grinned, then her smile faded. "I just had a terrible talk with the owners of these cabins." She recounted the conversation she had with them. "Not only do they not seem to care the least bit about Ashley's death, they are ready to try to pin it on Kyle if I say a word about what happened here. How can people be so awful?"

"Sounds like they should be at the top of the list of murder suspects." Sonia narrowed her eyes. "Perhaps they didn't want to wait until Ashley's contract ran out to be rid of her."

"That's a very good point." Nikki settled in one of the chairs at the table. "But that only makes things worse."

"Why is that?" Sonia handed a few treats to Princess, then a few to Coco.

"Because, if they are the ones that killed Ashley, then they are going to want to find someone to pin the murder on, and right now, Kyle seems to be on their radar and the easiest fall guy." Nikki's heart began to pound. "What if they succeed at making the police think he had something to do with it?"

A knock on the door made her jump.

"Nikki?" Kyle called out before knocking again.

"Come in, Kyle." Nikki stood up and began to pace as her brother stepped into the cabin.

"Hey, what's wrong?" Kyle watched her move back and forth. "You only pace when you're worried."

"I am worried." Nikki paused in front of him and looked into his eyes. "I'm worried about you, Kyle. Have you talked to the police?"

"Not recently." Kyle frowned. "Why?"

Pounding on the door of the cabin interrupted Nikki before she could continue.

"Who is knocking like that?" Sonia stood up from the table.

The pounding on the door sounded again. Nikki froze, unable to decide whether to answer or to pretend no one was inside. Coco and Princess made that decision for her, as they both began to bark at the door.

"It's the police." Kyle balled his hands into fists. "What if they're here to arrest me?"

"They can't do that, Kyle. You haven't done anything wrong." Nikki's heart pounded as she did her best to sound convincing. What if they did arrest him? What could she do to stop them? What could she do to help him? "You have to answer, Kyle. You have to cooperate with them, or it will make everything look worse."

"How can it look worse?" Kyle gulped back a groan, then reached for the door.

Nikki held her breath as he pulled it open. Conner and Schwitz stepped inside.

"We need to speak with you, Kyle." Conner pulled his hat off and tucked it under his arm.

"It's about the murder." Schwitz smiled, her eyebrows pinched together, and she rocked forward as if saying the word made her lose her balance.

"Of course, anything you need." Kyle shot a look in Nikki's direction, then looked back towards the officers.

"We need those." Conner pointed to Kyle's boots.

"And some spit." Schwitz pulled a plastic tube from her pocket, along with a wrapped cotton swab.

"Okay." Kyle took a slight step back. "I guess."

Nikki grabbed Kyle's arm and pulled him close. "You don't have to give a DNA sample if you don't want to."

"She's right. But we'll just get a warrant for it if you don't." Conner tapped his fingertips against his folded arm. "It will be such a waste of time."

"It's fine." Kyle shrugged. "I don't have anything to hide. Take my boots, take my spit, do you want a urine sample, too?"

Nikki clenched her teeth and tried to hold back her desire to chastise her brother. How could he joke at a time like this?

CHAPTER 7

*A*fter Kyle left for his cabin, Nikki pulled her phone out of her pocket.

"That's it, I'm calling Quinn."

"You haven't called him about all of this yet?" Sonia shook her head. "You should call him right away."

"I'm dialing now." Nikki cast her a brief smile then settled onto the couch. As she listened to the phone ring, she wondered if it might go to voicemail.

"Hi Nikki, how's the winter wonderland?"

"Hi Quinn, I hope I'm not interrupting anything." Nikki held her breath as she waited for him to respond. She was prepared to hang up if he indicated that she was bothering him in any way.

But she really didn't want to. Kyle needed all of the help that he could get.

"Not at all. I'm glad to hear from you. I thought maybe you would text me when you got to the cabin. I was starting to worry." Quinn scoffed. "I know, overreacting a little."

"I'm sorry. I just figured you were busy, and things got a little crazy last night." Nikki stroked Coco's fur as she considered how to tell him everything that had happened.

"Crazy?" A note of tension entered his voice. "What kind of resort is this?"

"Not that kind of crazy." Nikki described finding Ashley's body and the police's interest in Kyle as a suspect. "Today they took his boots and a DNA sample. I wasn't going to bother you with it, but I'm really starting to get concerned that he is their main suspect."

"If they collected those items then there is a good chance that he is the prime suspect." Quinn took a slow breath. "Okay Nikki, I know that this might upset you, but I have to ask. Are you absolutely certain that your brother had nothing to do with this murder?"

"Yes, I am certain!" She frowned. "He would never hurt anyone. He's not like that at all, Quinn."

"I understand. I don't know him well, so I had to ask. Now that I can assume he is innocent, there are some things you can do to help him. First, hire a lawyer."

"I don't think that's possible. All of the roads here are closed, and unless there is a lawyer staying in the resort that's willing to take on his case, I don't think that he's going to be able to do that." Nikki looked down into Coco's sad eyes. "This was supposed to be a family vacation. A nice getaway."

"I understand." Quinn paused, then continued. "Okay if you can't hire a lawyer, then he needs to be very careful about what he says, and how he says it to the police. If they want to close this case, and he looks good for the murder, then their main focus is going to be gathering enough evidence to implicate him. Hopefully, he has an alibi. If that's not possible, then you need to ensure that there isn't any evidence that will point the police in his direction. And hopefully there will be evidence to point in another direction."

"Thanks Quinn." Nikki shivered at the thought of her brother being the target of the police officers. "All of this is so helpful, and I know that you may feel a little conflicted giving me this advice."

"Not in the least. Nikki, I'm happy to help. I

only wish that I could be there with you to get you through all of this."

"Me too. Thanks Quinn." Nikki felt a bit over-whelmed by everything that had happened. She heard some noise in the background of the call, then Quinn sighed.

"I'm sorry, I have to take care of something, but if you need me, just call, okay?"

"Yes, I will. Thanks again." As Nikki ended the call, she couldn't help but wish he was there. But maybe if he couldn't be, she could play his part. She could be the detective that solved the case.

"Nikki, what did Quinn have to say?" Sonia sat down on the couch beside her. "I was trying not to eavesdrop, but I'm dying to know. Did he have any ideas to help Kyle?"

"Yes, he did have a few. I had one, too." Nikki looked over at Sonia. They'd become good friends, but would Sonia consider her plan too strange? "I want to investigate the murder. If I get stuck on something, I can always call Quinn for advice."

"I think that's the perfect idea." Sonia smiled. "Especially with those two fools on the case."

"I just think they could use a little help." Nikki rubbed her hands together, then held them out in front of the fire. The heat helped to calm her nerves.

"They said themselves that they would prefer to call in detectives, but with all of the roads being closed, there's no way that they can. So, how can they handle this case if they have no experience?"

"It certainly doesn't make me feel too confident in their abilities." Sonia stared at Nikki. "Oh honey, you look exhausted."

"I wasn't able to get much sleep last night. Every time I started to fall asleep, I thought about Ashley." Nikki wiped at her eyes, then blinked a few times. "I wish there was a way we could get to know her better. Maybe something about her life would point us in the right direction."

"I'm so sorry you had to see that, dear." Sonia picked Princess up and settled her in her lap. "I wish I had woken up to take Princess out. I am sorry, she usually wakes me up easily, but I must have been fast asleep after the drive."

"It's not your fault, Sonia. I'm glad you didn't take her out. I keep going over it in my mind. How long was Princess whimpering at the door? What if I slept through it, and she was trying to let me know that something was wrong outside? What if I could have stopped it?"

"Nikki, don't beat yourself up like that. Princess was whimpering right? She wasn't barking, or growling. If she really sensed something bad was happening outside, she would have made sure that one of us woke up. She's a very intuitive little pup." Sonia patted Princess. "Her bladder woke her up, that's all. I'm sure she was as surprised as you were to come across Ashley. But it's a good thing you both did. She might have been completely buried in the snow if she hadn't been found until morning."

"I guess you're right." Nikki nodded. "I want to find out what happened to her. I want to know who chased her through the snow, and why."

"Well, if that scarf has anything to do with it, we know that Betsy might have been involved." Sonia tipped her head in the direction of Betsy's cabin. "I haven't seen her come out of there all day. As nosy as she is, that's a little strange, don't you think?"

"I guess so." Nikki looked up at Sonia. "I have been considering going to Ashley's room, but I wasn't sure if it would be a good idea."

"It's a fine idea, as long as we don't get caught." Sonia leaned closer to her. "We can just take a peek around Ashley's room, find out what she's been up to lately, figure out who might have had a problem with her. What can it hurt?"

"I'm sure the police have already completed a

search of her room." Nikki tipped her head from side to side. "But breaking and entering?"

"We don't have to break. We could get the keycard." Sonia patted the top of Princess' head.

"How?" Nikki narrowed her eyes.

"They're all behind the desk, right? So, all we have to do is get one of us behind it." Sonia waved her hand. "Simple as pie."

"Simple as pie?" Nikki stared across the table at her. "It doesn't sound so simple to me."

"It can be, we just have to be careful." Sonia winked at her.

"I don't know about this." Nikki hesitated as she gazed at the wide smile on Sonia's face. "I don't want to get you into any trouble."

"Nikki, just because you are younger than me, doesn't mean you know best." Sonia locked her eyes to Nikki's. "I've been around a lot longer than you. I've had enough experience to know when to take a risk, and when not to. This is one of those times, when taking a risk is worth it. Every life is precious. There have been plenty of people in my life who would have described me as difficult and harsh at times, but my life still matters. Ashley deserves her justice, no matter what it takes to get it."

"You're right." Nikki took a deep breath. "She does deserve it."

"Good. Then, let's make a plan." Sonia smiled as she began to describe what she had in mind.

"That's perfect." Nikki grinned. "I think it'll work just fine. But I also think we both need to get some rest before we attempt it. Tomorrow morning?"

"Tomorrow morning." Sonia nodded. "I'm a little exhausted myself."

"I'm just going to take Coco out for a few minutes, would you like me to take Princess, too?" Nikki patted her thigh to call Coco over.

"Sure, that would be great. Thanks. I'm going to get changed then relax and read for a while." Sonia stopped at her suitcase, then headed for the bathroom.

Nikki opened the front door to let the dogs out and found a man right in front of her.

"Ken. What are you doing here?" She stared at him.

"I brought food." He held up two paper bags. "I got some food from the local fast food place. Luckily you can still get there on a snowmobile. I figured you two might be running low on grub." He held out the bags. "No strings attached, just cheese and grease."

"Nikki, who are you talking to?" Sonia stepped out of the bathroom with her robe tied tight around her waist. She froze when she saw Ken in the doorway. "Oh my, I didn't know we were having company."

"Sorry Sonia, Ken brought us some food." Nikki gestured to the bags.

"Blizzard supplies." Ken smiled at her. "I'll get out of your hair." He turned to walk away.

"Nonsense, you should stay and eat with us." Sonia motioned for him to come into the cabin. "What a kind gesture. I am quite hungry. Snack food just doesn't cut it. A good cheeseburger will hit just the right spot. Let me just get decent." She started towards the bathroom.

"You look fabulous to me," Ken called out as he stepped into the cabin.

Nikki raised an eyebrow and hid a smile. She excused herself to take the dogs out into the snow. As they chased each other around a bit she watched, and tried to relax. Maybe, the trip wasn't going as planned, but that didn't mean it wasn't beautiful. The wide-open blue sky above her was tinged with just enough gold to hint at the approaching sunset.

Curls of smoke drifted up out of the chimneys of the cabins. In the distance she could hear Christmas music playing from somewhere. Yes, it was quite beautiful. She was in the middle of a daydream about Quinn being there spending Christmas with them, when she was suddenly sprayed with snow.

"What's happening?" Nikki gasped as she stumbled back.

"Marshmallow, stop!" Max's voice bellowed. "Fluffy, you too!"

As the snow cleared, Nikki discovered two St. Bernards trouncing through the snow. One was clearly still a puppy, even though she was almost as big as Coco. As soon as Coco and Princess spotted them, the barking began. The four dogs greeted and sniffed each other. Nikki looked for any signs of animosity between them, but there wasn't any. Their tails wagged happily.

"I'm sorry, they don't usually take off like that. They must have smelled your dogs." Max leaned his hands on his knees as he tried to catch his breath.

"They're beautiful." Nikki smiled as she admired their brown and white coats and friendly personalities. "They're so big. Even Fluffy." Nikki laughed to herself as she realized that Marshmallow's head was bigger than Princess' whole body.

"Thanks. They are my pride and joy, that's for sure." Max sucked in another deep breath. "Do you have everything you need?"

"Yes, thank you." Nikki avoided his eyes.

"About this morning, I'm sorry. Gloria just goes off on her tangents and there's no stopping her." Max frowned. "I'm sure she upset you."

"I have no reason to be upset. My brother is innocent, and I know that. They're basing most of it on the size of his boot and a little animosity between them? It looks to me like you have a similar sized boot yourself." Nikki eyed his boot as he lifted one out of the snow.

"It's a common size." Max lowered it again, then looked up at her. "Just let the police do their job, and I'm sure we'll get to the bottom of it all. Let's go girls." He patted his knees to call the dogs. "Marshmallow, Fluffy!"

The St. Bernards reluctantly followed their owner's request. Nikki watched him go with some disdain. He was all apologies when Gloria wasn't around, but he didn't seem capable of standing up to her when she was present. Was that why there were only pictures of cats behind the front desk, and not his beloved St. Bernards?

When Nikki corralled the dogs back into the

cabin, she found Sonia and Ken seated by the fire with cheeseburgers and fries between them.

"There's some food left on the table." Sonia pointed to a bag, then laughed as Princess tried to climb up into her lap. "No, no, sweetie. You can't have food like this. It's no good for you."

"Oh, one fry won't hurt her." Ken held out a fry to Princess.

Nikki braced herself. She knew that Sonia had Princess on a very strict diet. She would never stand for her precious pup eating a french fry. But as she observed, Sonia smiled and blushed while she watched Ken feed Princess the fry.

Stunned, Nikki dug through the bag for a cheeseburger. Until she inhaled its aroma, she had no idea just how hungry she was. She took a huge bite, then sighed with satisfaction.

"I should be on my way." Ken stood up and walked towards the door.

"Thanks for the food, Ken." Sonia walked him to the door. "Stop by and say hi anytime."

"I'll do that." Ken winked at her, then waved to Nikki, before he left the cabin.

"Stop by and say hi anytime." Nikki fluttered her eyes and pretended to faint.

"Oh stop." Sonia grinned. "You're just enjoying this way too much."

"I'm not the one sharing french fries in front of the fireplace." Nikki smiled.

"Oh, poor Princess, eating junk food like that. I don't know what came over me. He's just such a charming guy, isn't he?"

"It sure seems that way." Nikki held back a few more words. The truth was, she felt a little uneasy around Ken. Maybe it was because he seemed too nice. Or maybe it was just his interest in Sonia that set off some alarms in her mind. She was just as protective of Sonia as she was of Kyle. She finished her burger, managed to brush her teeth, then collapsed into bed.

CHAPTER 8

The aroma of fresh coffee drew Nikki out of her dream. Somewhere between throwing snowballs at Quinn, and being aware of the cabin around her, she realized it was the most delicious smell. She blinked a few times, then looked towards the small kitchenette.

"Sonia, what are you up to?" Nikki sat up in bed.

"I just thought I'd make myself useful." Sonia smiled as she turned around with the pot of coffee in one hand. "We have a big day today, remember?"

"I think you're a little too excited about this." Nikki pushed back her blanket and climbed out of bed.

"I'm sorry, I just love an adventure." Sonia

poured coffee into two mugs, then set the pot back down. "Do you want cream or sugar?"

"Just a splash of milk." Nikki stretched her arms above her head. "Did you sleep well?"

"Yes, I did actually. I even took the dogs out this morning." Sonia offered a proud smile.

"Both of them?" Nikki glanced over at Coco who contentedly gnawed on a bone in front of the fireplace.

"Yes, Coco was a perfect gentleman." Sonia grabbed a few slices of toast out of the toaster. "I just made something quick, I hope you don't mind."

"Not at all." Nikki sat down at the table with her. "You didn't have to do all of this, I could have made breakfast."

"I don't mind. I needed something to keep me busy. I'm so excited about our plan today." Sonia spread some butter on her toast.

"I just hope it works. It wouldn't be good to get thrown out of the resort when the roads are impassable." Nikki took a sip of her coffee.

"Where is this pessimism coming from?" Sonia wagged her finger at her. "You have to think positive, remember?"

"I do." Nikki grinned. Normally, she was quite

the optimist. "All right, I'm sure it will go wonderfully."

"Good answer."

After they finished their breakfast they headed out. Along the way, Nikki questioned Sonia a few times about whether she was certain she wanted to do it.

"If you ask me one more time, I'm going to do it without you!" Sonia huffed and swung open the door to the lobby.

"All right, all right." Nikki followed after her, but ducked off to the side the moment she was inside. She skirted around the edge of the café and made her way to a dim hallway off to the side of the front desk.

"Yoohoo! Over here!" Sonia shuffled forward with Princess in her arms. Princess was the best dressed out of all of them, with a pink coat and boots to match.

"Yes?" Gloria turned to face her. She scrunched up her nose at the dog.

"Miss, something terrible has happened." Sonia sighed as she stood in front of Gloria. "I was just in my cabin, and you will not believe what I saw."

"What?" Gloria furrowed an eyebrow.

"It's just so terrible, I don't even know where to begin."

Nikki slid along the wall out of sight until she reached the edge of the desk. Then she crouched down. She held her breath as she wondered if Sonia would be able to pull this off. It crossed her mind yet again that she shouldn't be allowing this. But then again, she couldn't think of a way to stop Sonia once she had her mind set.

"Why don't you try beginning at the beginning?" Gloria frowned. "That's usually the best place."

"This morning I heard these soft little cries. It sounded just like kittens." Sonia sniffled.

"Kittens?" Gloria's tone sharpened. "Are you sure?"

"Yes. I tried to catch them, but they must have bolted every time I went near them. They are just so fast I never even got the chance to see them. It's so cold out. I just wanted to find them, but I got too cold. I thought maybe you would know of someone that could help." Sonia frowned. "Do you?"

"Oh yes, absolutely. We need to get out there right away. Let me call Max, he can bring the dogs, they're great at hunting down my kitties when they get out." Gloria pulled out her cell phone. "There's no time to waste, we can meet him out there."

As the pair headed for the door, Nikki braced herself. She hadn't expected such quick success, and now it was her turn to play her part. She slipped behind the desk, while keeping an eye towards the wall of windows. Without the falling snow to blur it, anyone could have a clear view of her activities. However, she didn't notice anyone looking in her direction. She grabbed a maintenance keycard, which she hoped would be programmed to open all of the cabin doors. She slid it into her pocket and then stepped out from behind the desk just as Max and the two St. Bernards bounded past the wall of windows. She took a sharp breath and ducked out of sight into the hallway. Once she thought it would be safe, she crept out towards the doors. The café was quiet, the lobby was empty, but she still felt as if someone was watching her.

As soon as she was outside, her phone buzzed with a text from Sonia.

Dropped off Princess. Meet you at Ashley's cabin. The Merners are cat hunting. We should have some time.

Nikki headed straight for Ashley's cabin. Kyle had been the one to tell her which one it was. He wanted to know why, but she avoided telling him. The last thing he needed was more suspicion thrown in his direction. When she reached the cabin, she found Sonia waiting for her.

"We might have fifteen, maybe twenty minutes before they realize there are no cats." Sonia smiled proudly. "I did good, didn't I?"

"Amazingly well!" Nikki nodded as she slid the keycard into the door.

"I once considered a career in acting." Sonia followed her into the cabin.

"Wow!" Nikki gazed at the assortment of owl statues, stuffed owls, and owl clocks, that decorated the space. "Creepy." Nikki drew back as the largest owl clock seemed to peer straight into her. His large eyes left her unsettled.

"I guess she was an owl person." Sonia chuckled. "Not my cup of tea for sure."

"But there's so many of them." Nikki shuddered. "And it feels like they're all staring at me."

"Well, it won't be long before someone is staring at us if we don't get a move on."

Nikki picked up a small, spiral notebook and flipped open the front cover. She noticed a list of dates and times along with the letter 'K'. Next to each date and time was a small note.

Cut through the courtyard.

It was the same note next to every date and time

that was listed. "Wow, this is about Kyle." She held up the notebook for Sonia to see. "This thing is filled with dates and times that Kyle cut through the courtyard. She must have been actively watching him multiple times a day."

"That's downright obsessive." Sonia shook her head. "I can't believe that she spent so much of her time doing that."

"Me either." Nikki set the notebook back down on the table where she found it. Then she picked it right back up again. She paged through it. The whole book seemed to be dedicated to Kyle. She flipped to the last page Ashley had written on. "This is from the day she was killed. She documented Kyle walking across the courtyard once, in the evening. There is a note scribbled underneath it. Fir Mt, ten PM." She snapped a picture of the page in the notebook. "It's a stretch, but it might explain why his boot print was found near the body. Maybe it was there from him crossing the courtyard earlier in the evening and the snow hadn't covered it yet." Nikki knew it was unlikely, but she thought there might be a slim chance that it was possible.

"Maybe." Sonia sorted through some papers stacked up on a small table beside the bed. "It sounds like she had a meeting with Kyle, too. We should ask him about that."

"Absolutely." Nikki narrowed her eyes.

"If she had any family, I'm not seeing any sign of it. No personal letters, no photographs. Not even a favorite CD." Sonia set the papers back down. "It was as if she worked hard not to have an attachment to anything."

"Anything, but these owls." Nikki passed her gaze across the collection once more. "How did she sleep in here with all of them staring at her?"

"Maybe it gave her some comfort." Sonia tipped her head from side to side. "If I didn't have Princess, I could have become quite lonely. Friends don't move in with you. The quiet can haunt you. Maybe she finds some comfort in the idea that she has an audience."

"Maybe." Nikki shuddered. "I'm not sure that I could ever find comfort in this particular audience. They seem like dust collectors, too." She scrunched up her nose as she looked them over. "Except for this one." She picked up one owl statue and looked at it. "This one has hardly any dust on it. Oh, the bottom opens up." She gasped as she peered inside. "Look at this." Nikki pulled out a small, silver digital camera. "She had it tucked away inside of there. If she hid it that well, I'm sure she had a reason."

"Are there pictures on it?" Sonia peered over her shoulder.

"Oh yes, I see a few." Nikki looked up towards the front door of the cabin. "We'd better get out of here, I thought I heard voices."

"Let's go." Sonia nodded, she led the way to the door. Once she stepped out, she took a quick glance around. Then she waved Nikki through.

Together they made their way back to their own cabin.

Nikki held tightly to the camera. She wondered what might be on it, and why Ashley had hidden it away. She guessed that she used it to document something, likely her brother's activities, but maybe along the way she caught a glimpse of her killer as well.

As soon as Nikki opened the cabin door, both dogs ran up to greet her, and Sonia.

"Hi babies." Nikki smiled and reached down to pet both of them. Then she hurried over to the table. "Let's see what pictures are on the camera."

"I hope they're of something more interesting than owls." Sonia rolled her eyes as she sat down beside her.

"Not much more interesting I'm afraid." Nikki sighed as she handed the camera over to Sonia. "Three photographs, each one as boring as the last. A box of blonde hair bleach left on top of a sink, a receipt from a toll booth, and a bottle of wine."

"Why take pictures of such odd things?" Sonia skimmed through the photographs.

"I have no idea. And they are the only three pictures on the camera. I guess all we found of use was that scribbled note. Hopefully, Kyle can tell us what the meeting was about. What a waste." Nikki sighed.

"I'm not sure it was a waste." Sonia put on her glasses and peered at the screen that Nikki pointed in her direction. "Obviously these pictures meant something to her."

"Or maybe she was just being nosy?" Nikki set the camera down. "It could mean nothing at all. Look at the way she documented every move that Kyle made. Of course, she didn't need to do that. There was no reason to be suspicious of him, or even to be giving him such a hard time, but she still did it. Maybe these pictures are of a mess that a guest left behind."

"She had a good reason in Kyle's case." Sonia lifted her chin as she looked at Nikki. "She wanted to get rid of your brother. He made her angry by refusing her advances. I'm betting she hoped that turning in that notebook to his boss at the ski lift would convince him to fire Kyle."

"She really was not a very nice person." Nikki sighed.

"I certainly haven't seen anything that proves otherwise." Sonia shook her head.

"I'm calling Kyle." Nikki stood up from the table. "I'll let the dogs out while I do."

"Nikki, don't be too hard on him. I'm sure he had a reason not to tell us about the meeting." Sonia frowned.

"It better be a good one." Nikki called the dogs to her, clipped their leashes on, then slid on her boots and coat. As she stepped outside, she dialed Kyle's number. It rang several times before he finally picked up.

"Hello?" His voice sounded a bit slurred.

"Kyle? Are you okay?" Nikki watched as the dogs kicked up snow in her direction.

"Fine, just sleepy. I was up late last night." Kyle cleared his throat. "What's up, Nikki?"

"Why did you meet with Ashley on Fir Mountain?" Nikki tightened her grip on the leashes and focused her attention on his answer.

"Huh? I didn't. What are you talking about?" He cleared his throat again.

"Kyle, don't keep things from me. I can't help you if you're not going to tell me everything." Frustration snapped through her as she felt the desire to force her brother to tell her the truth. He was generally an honest person, but there were times that he could stretch the truth or be evasive.

"I'm not keeping anything from you. I have no idea what you're talking about, Nikki." He sighed. "What did you find?"

"Kyle, you're in a lot of trouble. You know that, right?" Nikki fought to keep annoyance out of her voice.

"Of course I know that, Nikki. You're not the one the police are after, are you? I couldn't sleep last night, because I kept waiting for them to come through the door and arrest me. Look, if you're just going to argue with me, I'm going to go. I need some more sleep."

"Kyle, I'm sorry about how stressed you are, but I'm just trying to help you. Are you sure you didn't plan to meet Ashley at Fir Mountain?" Nikki tugged the dogs back away from a few guests that glided through the courtyard on skis.

"Yes, I'm sure." He hung up the phone.

Nikki winced as she heard the phone cut off. She knew that he was upset with her, but she was worried about him. Was he telling the truth about not having a meeting with Ashley? If so, why did Ashley write that note? Frustrated, she guided the dogs back towards the cabin. Before she reached the door, her cell phone began to ring. Maybe it was Kyle, maybe he was ready to tell the truth about what happened between him and Ashley. When she checked the number, it was one she didn't recognize.

"Hello?"

"Nikki, this is Gloria, I need to speak to Sonia right away, in fact, I'd like to speak to both of you. Please get to the lobby as soon as possible." Gloria sounded frazzled as she spoke.

"Gloria, is everything okay?" Nikki pushed open the door to the cabin.

"Just get here please!" Gloria hung up the phone.

Nikki frowned, a little put off by the woman's attitude, and still frustrated from her conversation with her brother.

"What did Kyle have to say?" Sonia set down her cup of coffee as Nikki stepped in with the dogs.

"Nothing unfortunately. He claims he has no idea about any meeting with Ashley. But that was

Gloria, she wants us to come to the lobby as soon as possible. She seems upset about something." Nikki brushed the snow off the dogs, then they raced straight for the fireplace to warm up. She checked on their food and drink supply, then turned to face Sonia. "I don't know what she wants, but it didn't sound pleasant."

"Do you think she knows?" Sonia's face grew pale.

"I'm not sure." Nikki's stomach twisted. "What if there are cameras around the front desk? I hadn't even considered that."

"Let's try not to think about it." Sonia winced. "Maybe they just want to talk to us about the investigation."

"Maybe." Nikki waited for Sonia to get into her coat and boots. "I just hope that Kyle is telling me everything relevant. What if he is hiding something from us?"

"You know your brother, Nikki, do you really think he could be involved in Ashley's murder?" Sonia gave Princess a quick cuddle then stepped through the door that Nikki held open.

"No, absolutely not. But he does have a talent for getting himself into messes." She pushed the door closed behind them. "Nothing like this, though."

"Just have faith in him, Nikki. If he isn't telling you everything, I am sure he has a good reason." Sonia fell into step beside her.

"Maybe." Nikki took a deep breath and tried to focus on what Gloria might want with them. If she did know that she and Sonia had been inside Ashley's cabin, what would happen next?

CHAPTER 9

The sight of the police snowmobiles parked outside the lobby sent an icy shiver through Nikki. She fought the desire to turn around and run the other way. With her mind still on her conversation with Kyle, she hadn't really considered what it might be like if she was arrested. What defense could she offer? She and Sonia exchanged an anxious glance as Nikki pushed the door open and held it open for her. Conner and Schwitz stood on either side of Gloria, who appeared to be irate.

"I'm telling you right now, there are kittens out there somewhere. Sonia, finally!" Gloria placed her hands on her hips as she stared at the officers before her. "Tell these incompetent officers that you heard kittens crying."

"I did." Sonia frowned. "At least, I thought I did. But I think it may have actually just been the pipes in the cabin. They make funny sounds."

"Pipes?" Gloria spun around to face her. "Are you telling me we spent all morning searching through the snow, because of some pipes?"

"I'm sorry for the confusion. If you had heard what I heard, you would have thought they were kittens too, I swear." Sonia offered a sheepish shrug. "I'm just relieved that there weren't really kittens trapped out there in the snow."

"Yes, you're right, that is a relief." Gloria turned back to the officers. "I suppose you can go now."

"Actually, we're here for a reason, and it's not the kittens. We're here to speak to you." Conner crossed his arms as he stared at her. "We'd like to know where you were at the time of Ashley's death."

"Are you kidding me?" Gloria huffed as she stared at the two officers. "You want to speak to me as if I'm some kind of suspect?"

"We have been told that you had quite a few issues with the victim. We wouldn't be doing our jobs if we didn't speak to you about it." Conner pulled out his notepad. "So, can you tell me where you were at the time of Ashley's death?"

"I most certainly won't!" Gloria looked over her shoulder at her husband. "Max, do you hear this? They're questioning me like a criminal! Get the lawyer on the phone!"

"Yes Gloria." He sighed and picked up the phone at the desk. "What would you like me to tell him?"

"Didn't you just hear what I said?" Gloria rolled her eyes. "They can't make me answer their questions."

"Gloria, you're absolutely right." Schwitz placed her hand lightly on the woman's arm. "We can't force you to answer our questions. If you don't want to, we can go. But I thought you would be interested in solving this crime, so that the resort can get back to business as usual."

"I am interested in solving it. But you wasting your time, questioning me, or my husband, is not going to solve it." She swung her hand through the air. "Your incompetence is boundless!"

"Gloria!" Max's harsh tone cut through his wife's high-pitched anger. "That's enough!"

"Maybe there's somewhere more private we

could speak?" Schwitz suggested as a few more guests entered the lobby. "Mr. Merner, do you have an office?"

"Sure, it's in the back. Gloria, just go with them. We have nothing to hide." Max looked into Schwitz's eyes. "We had nothing to do with Ashley's death, but whatever we can do to help with the investigation, we are happy to."

"You seriously have zero backbone." Gloria rolled her eyes, but as the officers led her towards the office, she followed after them. Max hurried to the front desk to help the guests.

Nikki breathed a sigh of relief as she realized that she and Sonia hadn't been caught. As her mind spun with what might have happened if they had been, she wondered if she had made the right choice by going into Ashley's cabin. Maybe her brother wasn't the only one with a talent for getting into messes. As she started to turn back towards the front door of the lobby, she caught sight of a familiar face in the café.

"Isn't that Betsy?" Nikki took a step in her direction.

"Yes, I think it is." Sonia squinted. "Looks like she's enjoying coffee and a muffin."

"Maybe she'd like some company?" Nikki raised

an eyebrow and glanced over at Sonia.

"Maybe she would." Sonia nodded, then walked towards Betsy.

Nikki followed a few steps behind her. As they neared the table, Betsy looked up at them.

"Hi neighbors." She smiled. "Would you like to join me?"

"Sure, thanks." Nikki sat down in one of the empty chairs, while Sonia took the third.

"Crazy day, isn't it?" Betsy tilted her head in the direction of the front desk. "Gloria caused such a scene."

"Yes, she did." Nikki studied the woman across from her. "How are you holding up with all of this?"

"With all of what?" Betsy lowered her voice and leaned across the table towards both of them. "Do you mean the murder?"

"Yes," Nikki whispered in return, though no one else was close enough to hear their conversation.

"I just don't know what to think. Ashley was such a sweetheart. Who would want to hurt someone like that?" Betsy pursed her lips.

"A sweetheart?" Nikki repeated as she stared at her.

"Oh sure, she told me all about the farm she used to live on. She was a horse person you know.

She loved riding horses. But she had to give all of that up when she lost her farm." Betsy sighed. "She was heartbroken."

"She told you all this?" Sonia's eyes widened.

"Yes, of course. We talked quite a bit. She would share a cup of coffee with me when she did her daily tidying. I think she was a little lonely. Especially considering how awful Gloria and Max treated her." Betsy shot a brief glare in Max's direction, then took another bite of her muffin.

"How did they treat her awful?" Nikki smiled as a waitress brought both her and Sonia a muffin and a cup of coffee. "Thank you."

"Oh, they bullied her so much. She had certain ways she liked to do things, and they would just argue with her every step of the way. It must have been so frustrating for her." Betsy shook her head. "She said they didn't want her here and no matter what she did they were always unhappy. They even threatened her more than once." She picked up her coffee and took a big swallow, then coughed a bit before continuing. "I told her she shouldn't let them treat her like that. She was too good of a person." She looked up as a man entered the café. "Brent, over here." Betsy waved. Nikki looked at the man walking towards them. She recognized him instantly. He was the man from the gas station. "This is Brent, he is also staying in one of the cabins. This is Sonia and Nikki." Betsy gestured to them.

"Nice to meet you, ladies." Brent smiled.

Nikki looked into his green eyes and was surprised that he didn't seem to recognize her. Neither of them acknowledged seeing each other at the gas station.

"Are you ready, Betsy." Brent gestured for the door.

"I am." Betsy finished the last bite of her muffin. "I'm off, we have a ski lesson to attend. It is so much cheaper as a pair. Enjoy your muffins, ladies, they are delicious."

Nikki watched them go, a bit too stunned to even say goodbye.

"I ran into Brent at the gas station on the way here." She looked at Sonia. "The one that we stopped at just before getting here."

"You did?" Sonia's eyes widened.

"That was weird, he didn't seem to recognize me."

"It was, but maybe he will next time." Sonia shrugged. "You couldn't have spent much time together at the gas station."

"You're right." Nikki nodded. "What Betsy said was interesting."

"She is the first person to describe Ashley as if she was a good person." Sonia shook her head. "We learned more about her in a few minutes than we have this whole time."

"And quite a bit about the Merners." Nikki watched as Max smiled at the next guest who stepped up to the desk. He had to be worried about Gloria in the office with the police officers, and yet he didn't show it. He was a good actor. "Perhaps those two are hiding a lot more than we thought."

"The way Gloria reacted just seemed so over the top." Sonia narrowed her eyes. "Almost theatrical."

"Maybe she thought she could throw the police off her trail by being so offended by their questioning." Nikki nodded slowly. "I think that's definitely a possibility."

"I think she's hiding something." Sonia nodded.

"Maybe it's time we took a look inside the owners' cabin." Nikki looked over at Sonia. "We can just peek in through some of the windows, since we know they're busy with the police and guests right now."

"I think that's a good idea, but we need a cover

story in case we are caught out there. The cabin is out of the way, but it is on the way to the slopes."

Nikki shifted her gaze towards the skis that lined the walls. She had skied many times with her family, her father's brother used to live near the mountains and they would often visit and go skiing.

"Do you know how to ski?"

"Sure, I used to ski every year. Let's gear up!" Sonia smiled.

Once they had everything they needed, Nikki led the way towards the Merners' cabin. In order to get to it, they had to pass by Ashley's cabin. Nikki glanced in the direction of the cabin, and wondered if she might have left anything behind that could prove she was there. The thought left her more chilled than the cold wind that blew against her cheeks. As she slowed down, she noticed a figure at the rear corner of Ashley's cabin.

"Who is that?" Nikki squinted through her goggles as the figure slid along the side of Ashley's cabin. "He has no business being there."

"I don't know, I can't tell from here. Do you want to try to get closer?" Sonia leaned forward. "You're right, it does look like a man."

"Let's just veer towards the cabin. We don't want to get too close. It could just be a guest with some morbid curiosity." Nikki shifted her path towards the cabin. As she did, the figure beside the cabin, suddenly bolted. He launched down a trail beside the cabin. Nikki's heart skipped a beat as she realized that he was going to get away without them having a chance to get an idea of who he was, or why he was by the cabin.

"I'm going after him!" Nikki glanced over at Sonia as she dug her ski poles into the snow.

"I'm going with you." Sonia lined up behind her.

"Stay close, Sonia." Nikki bent forward and launched down the same path the man had traveled down.

"I'll be right behind you." Sonia pushed off with her ski poles.

As Nikki skied down the trail, she felt a sudden lurch in her stomach. Even though she'd been skiing many times in her life, she always felt strange when she began to slide across the snow. Within a matter of seconds, she began to pick up speed. The farther she traveled down the hill, the more uneasy she felt. She tried to turn her skis in to slow herself down, but it seemed as if she picked up speed instead. Her heart raced as she wondered if she had made the wrong decision by going after the person in the ski mask. Of course, he was wearing a ski mask, it was a ski slope. She tried to slow herself down again. When it didn't work, she glanced over her shoulder to make sure that Sonia was still behind her.

Nikki spotted Sonia, farther up the hill, going at a much slower pace than she was. It looked as if she was in complete control. Nikki turned back to look at the path ahead of her just as she veered off onto another trail. A much steeper trail.

"Oh no!" Nikki gasped and tilted her skis again in an attempt to stop. In her panic she crossed them, and suddenly she began to tumble. The world spun as she rolled down the hill. Her ski poles were ripped out of her hands along the way.

When Nikki finally skidded to a stop, her body ached from the fall. There was no sharp pain to indicate a break. She took a breath and pushed her face up out of the snow. As she did, she noticed a figure that towered over her. He wore the same black ski mask that the man by Ashley's cabin had worn. Her eyes widened as he reached a gloved hand towards her.

"Are you okay?" He grabbed her hand and leaned down some. "Here, let me help you up."

Still dazed from the fall she allowed him to help her to her feet. "Thanks."

"You took quite a tumble there." He pulled his

goggles off to reveal deep blue eyes. "Are you all right?"

"Ken?" Nikki blinked as she stared at him. He was the person sneaking around Ashley's cabin? Her heart began to pound. "What are you doing out here?"

"Skiing." Ken narrowed his eyes. "What else?"

"Oh right, of course." Nikki cleared her throat. "Sorry, I guess I got a little jostled in that fall."

"Seems that way." Ken peered up the hill in the direction she had come from. "Is Sonia with you?"

"We got separated." Before Nikki went to find Sonia, she wanted to know what Ken was up to. "Did you know her?"

"Who?" Ken glanced back at her.

"Ashley. The woman who was killed. I saw you near her cabin." Nikki's heart skipped a beat as he gazed straight into her eyes.

"Did you?" Ken adjusted his ski poles in the snow.

"I only met her once." Nikki infused her voice with confidence, despite the sudden awareness that flooded through her. She was alone, on a rarely used trail, with a man who might just be a murderer.

"Well, I didn't know her. I only saw her a couple of times. I'm just here for a few days to enjoy the slopes. But I guess curiosity got the better of me. I thought I'd just take a look at her cabin. I mean, she died, right outside my door, practically." Ken sighed. "I've had a hard time sleeping. I keep wondering if I could have done something to help her. If only I'd known that she was in trouble."

"I understand that." Nikki pursed her lips and held back a wave of guilt. "I wish I had gone outside earlier. Maybe —" Her voice trailed off.

"Maybe she would still be here." Ken nodded, then pulled his goggles back down over his eyes. "No point in thinking about it, is there? She's gone now. You okay to get back to the cabins?"

"Yes, I'll be fine. Thanks." Nikki watched as he glided off down the remainder of the hill. By the time she reached the bottom of the slope, her mind was filled with curiosity about him. He'd taken the time to make sure that she was okay. She ran her gloved hands along her arms and assessed whether she really was okay. The aches that throbbed through her had already begun to fade. She looked back up the hill that she had tumbled down. The sight made her heartbeat quicken. She was very lucky to be okay. If Ken wanted to hurt her, he had every opportunity to do so. He could have killed her, and left her body behind. The police would have assumed that the fall had killed her. Instead, he made sure she was safe. Did murderers do that? She doubted it. But his explanation as to why he was near Ashley's cabin didn't ring completely true to her.

CHAPTER 10

*I*t took some time for Nikki to get back to the populated area of the ski slopes. As she neared it, she heard a shrill voice call out to her.

"Nikki! Nikki!" Sonia waved to her.

Nikki sighed with relief as she drank in the sight of the woman. She'd worried that she might have had trouble getting down the slope as well.

"Nikki, are you okay?" Sonia rushed towards her, though she was slowed down by the ski boots she wore.

"I'm fine." Nikki brushed a few chunks of snow from her jacket. "I took a tumble, but I was okay. Ken was there to help me."

"Ken?" Sonia's eyes widened.

"Yes, he was the one that we saw near Ashley's

cabin." Nikki frowned. "He claimed he was there because he hasn't been able to sleep. He keeps thinking about her murder."

"He could be telling the truth. I don't think either of us have been getting much sleep, have we?" Sonia met her eyes. "I think we should give him the benefit of the doubt."

"He does seem like a kind man." Nikki rolled her shoulders as an ache carried through them. "But I don't think we can rule out possible ill intentions. At this point, everyone needs to be a suspect."

"I know." Sonia frowned. "But he just seems like a nice man."

"Yes, he does." Nikki recalled the way he looked at her with concern in his eyes. "We didn't get a chance to check out the Merners' cabin, but it's getting late now. The dogs probably need to get out for a walk."

"Not to mention, you need to make sure you haven't done any serious damage to yourself." Sonia narrowed her eyes as she looked her over. "Do you want to go to the first aid office?"

"No, I'm fine. I promise." Nikki headed off in the direction of their cabin. After a quick glance over her shoulder to make sure that Sonia was still behind her, she quickened her pace. She felt an urgency to get back, though she wasn't sure why. A subtle pressure formed in her mind. What if Kyle had been arrested while she was gone? Worry for her brother filled her mind.

After they stowed their skis, Nikki snapped the leashes on the dogs, and led them outside. She could feel a few more aches, and while changing her socks to some dry ones, she had noticed some bruises. Sonia stepped outside behind her.

"Can I get any colder?" Sonia shivered as she took Princess' leash from her. "I can handle Princess."

"Are you sure?" Nikki glanced at her. "Wouldn't you rather be inside warming up?"

"I'm right where I want to be." Sonia held her gaze. "Until I know for sure that you're okay, you're going to have to get used to me being at your side."

"Thanks." Nikki smiled at her. She knew better than to argue. Sonia had one of the strongest wills she'd ever encountered. "At least the snow has slowed down." She took a deep breath of the crisp air.

"For the moment. The weather forecast calls for a few more inches today." Sonia shook her head. "It is tragic what happened. I've never felt more eager to get back to Dahlia." She reached down to pet Princess as she lingered near her side.

Nikki and Sonia turned at the sound of someone walking towards them. He was too far away to see his features, but he was too big to be Kyle or Ken. As he walked towards them Nikki noticed that his spiky, dark hair, reminded her of someone. All of a sudden, she recognized him as Brent, the man from the gas station and café.

"Hello, ladies." He smiled as he approached. "Oh, what beautiful dogs you have." He reached his hand down for Princess to sniff.

Princess gave a sharp yap, and ducked behind Sonia's legs.

"Sometimes she can be a little shy." Sonia cringed.

"I understand." Brent straightened up. "All of this must have put a damper on your vacation."

"Did you know Ashley?" Nikki asked.

"Ashley, well yes. I'd been here for a few days and she came to clean my cabin each day." He lowered his voice. "She wasn't very pleasant."

"No?" Nikki met his eyes. "Did you two have some trouble?"

"Not trouble exactly." Brent shook his head,

then lowered his voice further. "I caught her doing something she shouldn't have been."

"You did?" Sonia took a step closer to him. "What?"

"I don't want to speak ill of the dead." Brent grimaced, then took a breath. "I thought she was a bit nosy when she cleaned my cabin. I asked her why she looked at everything. She picked up my books, and asked me about where I came from. She said she considered herself a bit of a detective. That she liked to watch detective shows, and that people's things could tell a lot about a person. Well honestly, I didn't like it much." Brent cleared his throat. "I'm a private person."

"I wouldn't have either." Sonia narrowed her eyes. "Being a housekeeper doesn't give someone the right to dig through other peoples' things."

"I agree. Anyway, after that, I kept a closer eye on her. One day she was a bit late to show up, so I started looking for her through the windows. I was kind of hoping she wouldn't show. But I spotted her, at the cabin across from yours." He pointed towards Ken's cabin. "She opened the door, and went inside."

"To clean it?" Nikki shrugged as she listened to the man's story.

"No, not to clean it. That was the point. The day before I overheard the guy that's staying there arguing with Ashley about her coming into his cabin. He told her that he didn't want her in there at any time and he refused housekeeping. Ashley got pretty sharp with him and tried to insist, but he warned her that if he saw her near his cabin again, he would report her to the owners. I thought it was a little over the top myself. She might have been a little nosy, but she was a really great housekeeper. She cleaned things fast and well. She was only slowed down when she was being nosy." He took a deep breath and sighed. "Anyway, when I saw her at his cabin again, I thought it was strange. I didn't want to get her in trouble."

"Interesting. Maybe she was just being stubborn." Sonia tilted her head from side to side. "Ken told her no, and she didn't like to hear no."

"It's possible." Brent nodded. "She could be quite mean, though."

"Mean?" Nikki narrowed her eyes.

"Nothing, it was nothing." He smiled. "Enjoy your sweet pups. I'm going inside to get warm." He glanced at both of them and turned around to walk off.

Nikki looked towards Brent as he crossed the

snow to reach his cabin. He didn't remember her. But she remembered him.

"Interesting." Sonia glanced at Nikki.

"It seems like he knew quite a bit about Ashley."

"Including that she let herself into Ken's cabin. You know, I had assumed that Brent arrived here on the same day that we did, since I saw him at the gas station a couple of hours away." She reached down to rub Coco's back to ensure he wasn't getting too cold. "But it sounds like he's actually been here longer than we have."

"I need to get her inside, she's shivering." Sonia scooped up Princess.

"Let's all go in." Nikki looked towards Ken's cabin. She was tempted to walk over and knock on the door. Instead, she opened the door to their cabin for Sonia, and escorted Coco inside behind her.

As the dogs curled up near the fire to warm up, Nikki peeled off her coat and gloves. Then she pulled off her sweatshirt. Once she was down to her t-shirt, she examined her arms. There were a few bruises, but nothing too bad.

A knock on the door distracted her from her wounds.

"Who is it?" She walked over to the door.

"It's me, Kyle."

Nikki opened the door. "Hey bro." She smiled.

"Hey bro?" He raised an eyebrow. "Is that all you have to say to me?"

"What? Is something wrong?" She frowned as he walked past her.

"I had to hear from someone else about your fall down the hill. Why didn't you call me?" Kyle pulled off his jacket, then opened his arms to Coco as he bounded over to greet him.

"I'm fine, I didn't think you would hear about it to be honest. Did someone see me fall?" Nikki sat down on the couch beside him.

"Max did. He called me about it. Said he wanted to make sure that you were okay." He looked over at her. "Are you sure you're okay?"

"I'm fine, just a couple of bruises." Nikki sat back against the couch. "I actually wanted to talk to you about something."

"Okay, what is it?" Kyle smiled as Princess hopped up into his lap and lunged upward to lick his cheek.

"I know you said you didn't have a meeting with Ashley planned. But she had the note in her notebook. Which means that even if you didn't have it planned, she planned to meet someone on Fir Mountain." Nikki pulled out her phone to show him the picture. "My best guess is that maybe she planned to meet you, but didn't get to tell you about that plan before she was killed."

"She's nuts if she planned to meet anyone on Fir Mountain. It's roped off because it's too dangerous." Kyle scratched the top of Princess' head.

"Why is it so dangerous?" Sonia placed cups of hot cocoa in front of both of them, then joined them on the couch with her own cup in her hand.

"Thank you." Kyle smiled at Sonia. "It's dangerous because it's steep, but that's not the dangerous part. This time of year, there can be snow slides. Snow slides are like little avalanches. They don't make it down here to the resort, but if you're up on the mountain they can trap you. There are small crevices and caves that you can take shelter in, but if no one can get to you, then you just prolong your death." He grimaced.

"Yikes, that sounds terrible." Sonia clutched at her neck. "Could you imagine being trapped by the snow?"

"I'd rather not." Nikki frowned. "But I'm sure that doesn't happen all the time, right? Why would she plan to meet someone there? She's worked here long enough to know that it's a dangerous place. But she still planned a meeting there."

"It's dangerous, Nikki." Kyle locked his eyes to hers.

"You haven't worked here that long, though." Nikki shrugged. "I thought we could take a trip up there, just to see where she wanted to meet. Maybe she left something behind, some clue as to what happened to her."

"That is a terrifically bad idea." Kyle shook his head and gently placed Princess on the floor. "You're going to have to figure out what she was up to another way."

"We're running out of ways." Nikki frowned. "I just spoke with Brent, and he said he saw Ashley slip into Ken's cabin after Ken told her not to go in. Every time I think I have a lead, it reaches a dead end."

"You can't take what Brent says too seriously." Kyle stood up from the couch and walked over to the fire. His shoulders flexed, then slumped as his voice deepened. "He got into an argument with Ashley just a short time before she was killed."

"He did?" Nikki stood up as well. "Why didn't I know about this?"

"I guess, I hadn't thought about it. It was one of those things I did my best not to get in the middle of, it was better for me to avoid it." Kyle shrugged and glanced over his shoulder at her. The tension in his features aged him by a few years.

"What did they argue about?" Nikki studied her brother.

"I have no idea. They were in the courtyard when I walked through. I expected Ashley to give me a hard time, but she was too busy hollering at Brent. Brent shouted right back. I got out of there as fast as I could." Kyle took a breath, then looked back at the fire. "Maybe we won't ever find out the truth, Nikki. Maybe this is just how things are going to be."

"Don't say that." Nikki stood up and walked over to him.

"Don't lose hope." Sonia took a sip of her cocoa. "We're both here for you."

"Thank you, Mrs. Whitter." He glanced at her, then frowned.

"Kyle, what's wrong?" Nikki peered at him closely. She could sense the defeat in the slump of his shoulders, and the tone of his voice.

"I don't like the way the police talked to me." Kyle brushed his hair away from his eyes and frowned. "Nikki, it isn't looking good. You've got to promise me that you'll tell Mom and Dad I had nothing to do with this. Can you promise me that?"

"Of course, I can." Nikki took his hand. "Kyle, don't worry. You're not going to get arrested for this."

"I'm pretty close." He narrowed his eyes. "They're breathing down my neck. Honestly, I feel like someone is following me."

"Kyle, I'm so sorry." Nikki slid one arm around his shoulders and tugged him close. "I know this is hard on you. But you can't give up. I know you didn't do this, and the police will see that, too."

"In a little town like this?" Kyle shook his head. "They just want to lock me up. I can see it in their eyes every time they look at me."

"We're not going to let that happen." Sonia stood up from the couch and set her cocoa on the coffee table. "Kyle, you're not alone here."

"I appreciate that. I really do." Kyle looked between the two of them. "But I can't just not worry. I'm sorry. This is my life on the line." He pulled away from Nikki and headed for the door. He paused in front of it, then looked back at Nikki. "Stay off Fir Mountain, got it?"

"Got it." She frowned as he stepped through the door.

CHAPTER 11

*L*ater that night, Nikki listened to the sound of Sonia's snoring. It wasn't intrusive, but a rather soothing snort that reminded her that someone else was there with her. At the moment, she appreciated that. As she toyed with her phone she wondered if it was too late to call Quinn. It wasn't quite eleven, but would it bother him?

"Would it bother me?" Nikki whispered the question at the dark ceiling. It wouldn't bother her one bit. She passed her finger over his name on her contact list and initiated the call. As she waited for the call to connect her mind spun. She'd never seen Kyle scared before. Not scared like this. Her younger brother was always the brave one, the daring one, the one that broke far too many bones.

But she'd seen fear in his eyes, heard it in his voice, and for the first time in her entire life, he looked small to her.

"Hi Nikki."

Quinn's voice drew her out of her troubling thoughts.

"Quinn." She smiled at the sound of his voice. It always surprised her just how much his voice affected her. "Sorry to call so late."

"I'm glad to hear your voice, anytime of the day or night." He paused a moment, then continued. "How's Kyle?"

"It's not going well, Quinn. The police here are really putting pressure on him. He's scared. I've never seen him this scared." Nikki kept her voice low, and Sonia continued to snore.

"Are you?"

"I hate to admit it, because I know everything will be fine, but yes I am a little. Ashley was keeping track of my brother's activities. She was trying to get him fired. The police have to see that as a good motive for him to be angry with her. He has no alibi." Nikki sighed. "I know how busy you are, Quinn, I appreciate you listening to me ramble."

"I don't think it's rambling. Honestly, I wish I could be there to help you. I thought about coming, but the roads are all still closed leading into the area."

"That's nice of you." Nikki's heart softened at the idea of him coming to her rescue. Maybe it was a little outdated, but it still felt nice to know that he wanted to be there to help. "I'm sure we can handle it. I guess I'm just not sure what to do next."

"If I were there, I would focus on figuring out who might have had a better opportunity and motive than Kyle to commit the crime. Review the evidence at the crime scene. Nine times out of ten, the clue to solve the murder is right there from the start. It takes working that clue to get to the culprit." Quinn paused, called out some instructions to someone else, then continued. "I know you probably don't have access to any of the evidence from the scene, but you were the one to discover the body. You were the first one to see it."

"Yes, I was." Nikki closed her eyes as she recalled the sight of Ashley's body. "Thanks Quinn. This is all great advice."

"Then I hope you will listen to one last piece of advice." His tone hardened just enough to indicate how serious he was.

"Sure, what is it?"

"Get some sleep, Nikki. It's nearly impossible to

solve a crime when you're tired. It may seem impossible to rest with so much on your mind, but you have to try."

"I will." Nikki smiled to herself as her muscles relaxed and her mind began to slow. Talking to Quinn had eased the tension in her body. "Good night, Quinn."

"Good night, Nikki. Stay safe."

Nikki hung up the phone and set it on the bedside table. Moments later, something cold and wet pressed against her cheek. She jolted awake to discover that it hadn't been moments, it had been hours, and Coco had terrible morning breath.

"Morning Nikki." Sonia stretched her hands above her head before standing up from the edge of her bed. "Did you sleep okay?"

"Very well." Nikki smiled, though her brother's predicament weighed heavily on her. "You know what? We need to find out why one of Betsy's scarves was at the crime scene."

"You're right." Sonia headed for the kitchen. "I'll make us some coffee."

"I'm going to run the dogs outside. Maybe we'll even say good morning to Betsy." Nikki gathered the dogs and pulled on her coat, then stepped outside.

For once, there was no snow falling. The bright morning sun promised to begin to melt some of the snow that had piled up. As Nikki let the dogs roam as far as the leashes would allow, she edged closer to Betsy's cabin. As she got closer the door swung open.

"Hello there," Betsy called out and waved as she hurried over to Nikki. She was bundled up, complete with a thick, black scarf around her neck. "How are you this morning?"

"Doing okay, thanks." Nikki smiled in return. "And you?"

"Pretty good, glad to see the sun." Betsy took a deep breath, then released it in a sharp burst. "Still cold, though."

"Very." Nikki grinned. "Why aren't you wearing your colorful scarf?"

"You were right, it just wasn't warm enough." Betsy shook her head.

"Hey listen, I was wondering, did the police ever ask you about the scarf that was with Ashley's body?"

"Ouch, not a good morning conversation." Betsy shivered as she played with the scarf around her neck. "I told them, I gave it to her. She was always admiring it, and I wanted to give her something. So,

I offered her one of my handmade scarves. She seemed really touched that I did."

"That was very thoughtful of you." Nikki tightened her grasp on the dogs' leashes. Her eyes remained focused on the black scarf. Had she really replaced it just so she could be warmer, or was it her scarf that Princess found in the snow?

"Maybe. It does give me some comfort to think that I gave her a gift not long before she passed." Betsy shivered and then smiled. "It was good to see you this morning, I'm going to enjoy the warmth inside a little bit longer."

"You do that." Nikki grinned. "Maybe we could have coffee again sometime?" She took a step towards her.

"Sure, that would be nice." Betsy waved to her, then headed back to her cabin.

Nikki guided the dogs back towards the cabin. If Betsy was telling her the truth, then she had even less motive to kill Ashley. It didn't cross her off the list, but it certainly put her lower on it. When she stepped back into the cabin, she found Sonia waiting for her with a cup of coffee.

"How did it go? I saw you out there with her."

"She was sweet as sugar, as usual. She said she gave Ashley the scarf as a gift." Nikki shook her head. "I'm not sure if I believe her, but I am less inclined to think that she killed Ashley."

"Interesting." Sonia glanced at Nikki.

"I've been going over the evidence from the crime scene in my head. We can't figure out what the black plastic is right now, and the scarf has an explanation, but what about the boot print? If the boot print in the snow is one of their main pieces of evidence, then let's try to find someone with the same size boot."

"It will at least split their attention between Kyle and this other person."

"I doubt that Betsy or Gloria have the same size boot." Nikki frowned. "But Max might. I think we should start there."

"Then forget this coffee, let's go to the café and have some. I'm sure he'll be there. I've already set out breakfast for the pups." Sonia grabbed her coat and gloves.

"Good plan, not sure how we're going to get a good look at his boots, but it's worth a try." Nikki gave both dogs a good pet, then straightened up.

"I know how we can. I've seen that they both leave their boots by the front door and change into dress shoes. I guess they are concerned about presenting a certain image." Sonia tugged her boots on.

"I never noticed that." Nikki gazed at her with admiration. "Good observation."

"Thank you." Sonia smiled.

When Nikki and Sonia reached the lobby the smell of coffee and pastries filled the air. Nikki did her best to ignore the hunger that twisted her stomach into knots. But the pastries smelled so delicious she could barely resist.

"I'm starving." Sonia grabbed her hand and tugged her towards the café. "Let's eat. We need to look casual, right?"

"Yes, I guess we do." Nikki spotted Max as he rounded the corner from the hallway into the lobby. While Sonia ordered their coffee and pastries, Nikki watched Max as he walked over to the collection of snow boots by the front door. When he picked up a pair to put them on, she walked over to him.

"Going out to walk the dogs?" Nikki slid her phone out of her pocket.

"Yes." Max passed his gaze over her. "Why?"

"Oh, I was just wondering. Is this the time that you usually take them out? I thought maybe we could walk them together sometime." Nikki held her phone by her side, and ran her thumb across the screen. She could only hope that she had managed to open her camera.

"I suppose we could do that." Max shrugged. "Yes, this is the time." He picked up his boot, and slid it on to his foot. She pressed the button on the side of her phone to take a series of pictures as the sole of his boot tilted into the air. She did the same as he put on the other boot.

"I'll keep that in mind for tomorrow." Nikki smiled at him, then headed back over to the table that Sonia had chosen.

"Did you get it?" Sonia hissed as Nikki sat down across from her.

"I'm not sure, yet." Nikki skimmed through the pictures on her phone, then smiled. "Yes, he has the same size boot!" She snapped her fingers. "It certainly could have been him. He had a problem with Ashley, maybe he saw this as the best way to take care of it. I'm going to let the officers know." She began to send a text on her phone.

"Wait." Sonia placed her hand on Nikki's arm. "Don't just yet." She looked into the young woman's eyes. "Let's keep this information to ourselves for just a little while."

"What? Why?" Nikki frowned. "The sooner they get this information, the sooner they can turn their attention away from Kyle."

"You're assuming that they are good at their job. But they benefit from the resort being here. If one of the owners is found to be the killer, do you really think they are going to be eager to make that arrest? It could cost them, and this entire area, a whole lot of money." Sonia frowned. "Call me cynical, but I'm not sure we should trust those two. I think we need to find some more solid evidence that proves beyond a doubt that Max is the killer, before we go to the police."

"You're right." Nikki tucked her phone back into her pocket. "There has to be something more that can point them in his direction."

"Maybe it's time we got a little buddy buddy with Gloria. She seems the type to get loose lips when she drinks." Sonia took a sip of her coffee. "But it will have to be you, not me. After the kitten incident, she's given me nothing but suspicious looks."

"Me?" Nikki bit into her bottom lip, then shook her head. "I'm not sure that I could get her to talk."

"I'm sure that you can." Sonia sat forward and looked into her eyes. "Nikki, you're a brilliant, young woman. You know that, don't you?"

"Thanks Sonia, but I'm not sure that she'd believe me. We've had some tense moments, too." Nikki frowned and glanced in the direction of the front desk. Gloria shot their table a brief look of animosity. Nikki looked back at Sonia. "I'm not sure that it's going to work."

"All you can do is try, dear." Sonia picked up her danish. "Either way, you might find out something new about Gloria."

"Good point." Nikki took a deep breath, then looked back in Gloria's direction.

Nikki spent the rest of the morning and most of the afternoon looking into Gloria. What she discovered surprised her.

"Sonia, Gloria has owned a cat sanctuary in the past. She really does have a passion for felines." Nikki narrowed her eyes as she read over a recent article about her. "It sounds like there was a bit of a scandal over the sanctuary. Maybe that's what really led to the purchase of the resort. A change of pace I suppose."

"What kind of scandal?" Sonia peered over her shoulder.

"A group of people protested against the sanctuary, claiming that Gloria didn't take good enough care of the cats. She lost it on them and was charged with assault, but the charges were dropped." Nikki glanced over at Sonia. "I couldn't imagine her not taking care of the cats properly. She seems to adore them when she speaks about them. But I guess there is possibly a history of violence, or at least a temper, don't you think?"

"Yes, I do think. And I'm sure that Ashley was pushing all of her buttons. She seemed like the type of woman to try to stir up trouble wherever she could." Sonia clucked her tongue. "I bet the two got into something very heated, and Max had to finish off the job."

"I guess I'll try to find out." Nikki glanced at her watch. "Gloria should be home by now. I'm going to head over to their cabin. Luckily, you brought with some wine to give to your niece. Are you sure it's ok if I take a bottle?"

"Of course, text me if you need anything at all." Sonia walked her to the door. "I'll be on call."

"Don't worry, now that I know a little more about Gloria, I'm sure that I can do this." Nikki blew Coco and Princess a kiss, then zipped up her coat. As she walked across the courtyard in the direction of the Merners' cabin, she shivered. The temperature had dropped quite a bit. Luckily, there was no more snow. Hopefully, the road crews would make some progress at clearing the roads. She guessed that things could easily go sideways after her conversation with Gloria. When she knocked on the door, a quick rush of fear almost drove her back from it. This is for Kyle, she reminded herself, and knocked again.

The door swung open, and Gloria gazed at her, her eyes narrowed and her forehead wrinkled.

"Hi Gloria." Nikki smiled as she held up the bottle of wine in her hand. "I brought something for you. Well, for us."

"What's this about?" Gloria's lips pinched together in annoyance.

"I just wanted to apologize. I know things got a little out of hand between us. Everything is tense, because of Kyle's involvement in the investigation. But we're all stuck here together in this snow, and I hate for tension to be in the air." Nikki offered her the bottle of wine. "I thought maybe we could have a drink together and just start over. Maybe I could meet your cats?"

"Oh yes." Gloria smiled at the mention of her cats. "They do love having visitors." She glanced past her. "No tag-a-longs? I make Max keep his dogs in another cabin, because they scare my kitties." She narrowed her eyes. "Brute things they are."

"No, the dogs are at home." Nikki clenched her teeth against the words that she wanted to speak. The dogs lived in another cabin? Did Max live with them?

"In that case, come right in. I'll get us some glasses." Gloria held the door open for Nikki.

Nikki stepped inside to discover a luxurious interior. It was far nicer than any of the cabins she'd seen so far, and at least twice the size of them. The furniture all looked far too expensive to sit on, and the décor appeared to be handpicked by a magazine editor. Even the fireplace looked too perfect to ever use. She lingered just inside the door and wondered if she'd made a mistake. How could she fit in, in a place like this? How could she find anything in common with a woman like Gloria?

CHAPTER 12

*N*ikki unzipped her coat as she began to sweat. She wondered if she had gotten herself in over her head.

"Here are some glasses." Gloria set them down on the coffee table along with a cheese platter. "I just love cheese platters. I share them with my kitties. Well, the crackers, not the cheese."

Nikki didn't see any evidence of cats in the cabin. She stared at Gloria for a moment and wondered if she might have imaginary cats.

"Your home is beautiful. Impeccable." Nikki smiled.

"Oh please." Gloria waved her hand. "Ever since Ashley passed away it's been a wreck. She used to come in twice a day. Another staff member has been doing the housekeeping, but they aren't very good. I've been trying to get someone else, but the roads are all blocked, so there's not much chance of that in the next few days. The fur is absolutely everywhere." She scrunched up her nose in disgust.

Nikki eased herself down on the edge of a couch that appeared to be upholstered in pure silk, then looked back at Gloria.

"I don't see any fur."

"My kitties don't shed too much, but when I see it, it drives me crazy." Gloria cleared her throat, then called out in a high-pitched tone, "Tut, tut, tut, tut, babies!"

Nikki raised an eyebrow at the call, and at the face that Gloria made as she called to her cats. An instant later she heard a rush of paws. She gasped as cats bolted out from under the couch, and from the corners of the cabin. She lifted her feet up just as one buzzed past her. They were all short hair cats, their fur all different shades, and colors. Some of the cats were small, while others were large enough to be of a unique breed. All seemed intent on getting into Gloria's lap before any of the others could. As the cats struggled to gain affection from their owner, Nikki admired their beauty.

"They are wonderful. They all look so healthy."

"They are. I spend quite a bit on the vet." Gloria grinned as one of the cats dragged its tail across her face. "They're so loving."

"I see that." Nikki smiled. "Thanks for introducing them to me." She opened the wine bottle and poured them each a big glass. "It must be tough starting out new here."

"It hasn't been too bad. At least, not until now. Max and I just wanted a place we could call our own. But there have been struggles." Gloria sighed, then took a big swallow of her wine.

"I bet. I know that Ashley had her own way of doing things." Nikki watched Gloria's reaction closely.

"That's putting it lightly. I have never met a more difficult woman." Gloria gulped down more wine.

"That must have been so frustrating for you. Here you are, starting a new chapter, a fresh opportunity to succeed, and she wanted to fight you every step of the way." Nikki lowered her voice. "It would have driven me crazy, to be honest. I can have quite a temper when someone stands in my way."

"Oh, me too, me too." Gloria held up her glass and clinked it against Nikki's. "Nothing stops me once I lose it. Whoever is in my way has hell to pay." She grinned, then drank the remainder of the wine in her glass.

Nikki was quick to fill it. "Who could blame you? She stood between you and a peaceful life. At least, until now, right?"

"Right." Gloria giggled as she picked up her glass again. "She's not a problem anymore. Bye-bye, Ashley." She wiggled her fingers in the air.

The front door swung open, and the cats scattered so fast that Nikki gasped and drew her feet up off the floor. She'd barely had a chance to look in his direction before Max's sharp tone reached her ears.

"Gloria! What have I told you about having company?"

"Oh hush." Gloria rolled her eyes. "You're always with those dogs, I need someone to talk to."

"What's going on here?" Max snatched the empty bottle of wine up. "Did you drink all this?" He frowned and slammed the bottle back down on the coffee table.

"No, no, of course not. Nikki had some, too. Right Nikki?" Gloria hiccoughed.

"Yes, I did." Nikki twisted the stem of her wine glass. She'd only drank a few sips of wine, but Gloria didn't know that. Her eyes remained glued to

Max as his anger continued to grow. "We were just having a nice evening, Max, that's all."

"How could you be so stupid, Gloria?" Max glared at her. "She got you drunk on purpose. What did you tell her?"

"She wouldn't do that." Gloria waved her hand and laughed. "Would you, Nikki?" She stared at Nikki as she swayed back and forth on the couch.

"Of course not." Nikki stood up and started for the door. "I should go."

"Wait a minute." Max stepped in front of her. "Whatever she said to you, I'd better not hear it repeated, understand?"

Nikki stared into Max's eyes as her heart pounded. This man wasn't the timid man she had seen before.

"I understand, but she didn't say anything." Nikki shivered. The fury in his eyes was so potent that it darkened their color. She sensed that if he'd had the freedom to do so, he would have picked her up and thrown her right out of the cabin. At her size, he could easily do it.

"You need to leave." Max snapped his hand towards the door.

"Okay." Nikki swallowed back a few sharp words as she hurried to the door. Yes, she'd like to tell him exactly what she thought of him, but she wasn't going to tempt a man who was likely a murderer.

As soon as Nikki was outside in the freezing cold, she realized her mistake. As long as Max and Gloria thought that she suspected them, they would be even more determined to make sure that the murder was blamed on Kyle. She turned back to the door and took a breath. Then she knocked firmly on it.

Max ripped the door open.

"What is it?"

"Please tell Gloria I had a nice time. I'm not sure what's upset you, Max, if I've offended you some-how, I'm sorry about that. I just wanted to apolo-gize." Nikki looked straight into his eyes. "I just wanted to spend some time with Gloria. We had a nice time."

"You came to apologize?" Max smiled at her, though his eyes remained darkened by the tension in his gaze. "How nice." He closed the door again. She heard the lock slide into place. As she stared at the door a moment longer, she felt a sense of doom rise within her. What if Max decided that she was a problem, too?

Not long after Nikki left, Sonia settled on the couch with Princess in her lap. Not to be ignored, Coco crawled up onto the couch beside her and set his head on her knee.

"Aw, you're just a charmer." Sonia smiled as she gave him a light pet. "Hopefully, this doesn't get you in trouble when you go back home. I'll never understand why people don't want their pets on their furniture." She scratched under his chin.

Abruptly, Coco launched towards the door. His sharp barks made Sonia's heart skip a beat. Princess jumped down next, her yaps barely audible as Coco continued to bark.

Between the two of them, they almost drowned out the sound of a knock on the door.

"Sonia, are you in there?"

"Just a minute, Ken." Sonia shooed the dogs away from the door, then pulled it open.

"Sorry, I didn't mean to cause so much chaos." Ken offered her a sheepish smile that softened his eyes.

"Don't worry, they just compete to see who has the louder bark. Don't tell Princess, but Coco wins.

Of course, Princess just keeps trying." Sonia laughed as she scooped the dog up into her arms.

"Maybe one day, Princess." Ken winked at her. "Do you mind if I come in? It's freezing out here."

"Of course." Sonia stepped aside to let him in, then closed the door behind him. "What are you doing out and about in the cold?"

"I felt a little restless. I thought maybe you'd like some company." Ken shrugged, then looked into her eyes. "Would you?"

"Absolutely." Sonia smiled and led him towards the couch. "You get comfortable, and I'll get us some wine."

"Oh, that sounds great." He pulled off his scarf, then his coat. "Something to warm me up."

"Absolutely." Sonia returned with two glasses and a bottle of wine. "At least it stopped snowing, hmm?"

"We're supposed to get more tonight." Ken winced. "Hopefully not. I heard the roads might be clear by tomorrow."

"What will you do then?" Sonia poured them both a glass of wine. "Are you going to move on?"

"No, I don't think so. I'll probably wait out the holiday traffic here." Ken shrugged as he held out his hands to the fire. "It's as good a place as any."

Ken took his glass of wine from Sonia. He held the glass by the stem, held it up to the light and examined it, then swirled the wine, sniffed the aroma, and took a sip. He swished the wine in his mouth then swallowed.

"Is it okay?" Sonia raised an eyebrow.

"Sure is." Ken stretched his legs out until his boots were propped up against the brick of the fireplace. "Thanks for sharing it with me."

"Thanks for the company." Sonia set the bottle down. "What are you doing out here all alone, Ken?"

He took a slow sip of his wine, stared at the flames, then shrugged.

"Nowhere else to be I suppose. I was down south, and I just had the urge to be in the cold for Christmas. I had no one to spend it with, so I figured why not go somewhere new?" Ken shook his head as he looked towards the window where fresh snow fell. "Guess I didn't think about getting snowed in."

"Neither did we." Sonia laughed. "I wasn't even supposed to be here, you know. I was supposed to be with my niece. But the roads were blocked, so Nikki was kind enough to let me stay with her."

"What's the deal with you two?" Ken looked over at her. "Is she your granddaughter?"

"No." Sonia blushed as she recalled just how old she was. Of course, this fine-looking gentleman couldn't be flirting with her. Could he? "She's a friend of mine. My dog walker and pet sitter, actually, but we've become quite close."

"That's nice." Ken gazed at her. "It's good to have someone that you can trust. I suppose she tells you everything?"

"We're close." Sonia nodded. "What about your friends? Do you have any that are missing you for the holidays?"

"No, no one." Ken stretched his arms above his head. When he relaxed them again, one sprawled along the length of the couch cushion just behind her. "I lost touch with everyone over the years. One of the drawbacks of always traveling for work. Now that I'm retired, I still can't stay in one place long enough to make many connections."

"I'm sorry." Sonia studied the lines of his face, and the droop of his lips. She sensed sadness hidden behind his tough facade. "That must be a difficult way to live."

"Most of the time it's not. When you don't have anyone, you can't miss anyone, which is actually very liberating. It's when I meet someone spectacular, that's when it's difficult to move on." Ken's arm slid forward until his fingertips curled around her shoulder.

Sonia's heartbeat quickened in response to the touch. She met his eyes as he turned towards her.

"Ken?"

"Someone like you, Sonia." He looked into her eyes. "Someone so remarkable."

"Oh, I'm not very remarkable." Sonia laughed as her heart raced.

"Yes, you are. The way the fire dances in your eyes, you look so beautiful." Ken sat back against the couch again. "I'm a little rusty when it comes to romance."

"You don't seem very rusty." Sonia smiled. "But I think I've had enough wine."

"Sonia, I'm sorry if I've made you uncomfortable." Ken closed his hand over hers. "It's been so long since I got to share the company of a beautiful woman. I forgot my manners."

"I think maybe you should go." Sonia stood up from the couch. She could hear Princess scratching at the door. She glanced at her watch and realized that almost two hours had passed. She checked her phone to be sure she hadn't missed a call or text from Nikki. Relieved that she hadn't, she looked back up to find Ken's eyes locked on her.

"Sonia, please don't be upset with me." Ken stood up as well.

"I'm not." Sonia smiled as she walked with him to the door. "Not at all." She ignored a subtle flutter in her chest. It had been some time since she'd had her last romantic encounter. "You've brightened my holidays, Ken. I hope you have a good evening."

"You, as well." Ken gazed into her eyes a moment longer before he stepped out through the door.

CHAPTER 13

$\mathcal{N}$ikki shivered as an icy wind threatened to cut through her jacket. It was easy for her to assume that it was Max who was the killer. She didn't like the way he looked at her, or spoke to her. She didn't like the way he spoke to his wife. But none of those things were evidence, or any kind of proof that he was the killer. She reviewed in her mind the evidence found at the crime scene, again. Yes, he had the same sized boot. But so did Kyle. There was an explanation for the boot print, and the scarf. But what about the broken plastic in the snow? What could it be? She racked her mind for anything that would be similar in color and density that Ashley had on her body. She couldn't place anything. What about Max? Nothing came to mind, either. Suddenly she recalled Brent's purchase at the gas station. Who needed sunglasses in a snowstorm?

"What if it wasn't Max?" Nikki's heart skipped a beat as she neared the cabin. What if it was Brent? A scenario played through her mind. Brent, enraged at Ashley's invasion of his space, confronts her. She, with her spirited attitude, fought back. In the struggle, his sunglasses fell out of his pocket, his boot crushed them. Maybe that was what the argument was about, but this time it got out of hand. She bit into her bottom lip as she shivered against the cold weather. The shiver reminded her of the way she felt the first time she saw Brent. Uneasy. But another person came to mind, Ken. What if what Brent said was true and Ashley really did go into Ken's cabin against his wishes? Maybe it was Ken's goggles that were crushed in the snow? He had mentioned that he needed to buy a new pair.

The door of the cabin swung open, and Nikki nearly walked right into Ken as he stepped out.

"Oh, excuse me!" Ken stepped to the side before he could collide with her. "We just keep running into each other." He chuckled.

"What are you doing here?" Nikki asked.

"Ken was just keeping me company for a little while." Sonia smiled.

"He was?" Nikki cleared her throat as she realized she was being a bit rude. She was so surprised to see him, right after she'd been entertaining the idea that he might be a murderer. "I'm sorry, Ken. I'd just like to get inside, it's so cold out here."

"You're right, it is." He zipped up his coat and pulled the hood low.

"Where did you say you were from?" Nikki locked her eyes to his.

"I didn't." He looked away, towards the mountains.

"Ken is a traveler." Sonia volunteered, and gave his arm a light pat. "Good night, Ken."

"Good night, Sonia." He bowed his head to her, then walked off into the snow.

"Get in here before you freeze." Sonia grabbed Nikki's hand and pulled her through the door of the cabin.

"It is so cold!" Nikki shivered and after greeting Coco and Princess she headed straight for the fireplace with the dogs behind her. As she passed the coffee table, she noticed two wine glasses, and a half-empty bottle of wine. "Sonia, did you have wine with him?"

"I sure did." Sonia grinned and joined Nikki by the fireplace.

"And?

"And it was nice." Sonia wiggled her eyebrows. "How did you go with Gloria?"

"It left me feeling a bit frazzled. Max came home while I was with Gloria and things got pretty heated." She recounted her confrontation with him. "He was so different to the person we originally met."

"Oh no, Nikki, are you okay?" Sonia scowled. "How dare he. He didn't hurt you, did he?"

"No, he didn't, but I think he might have liked to." Nikki knelt down in front of the fireplace and held out her hands to warm them. The flicker of the flames reflected on something that caught her eye. "What's this?" She leaned closer to the bricks that surrounded the fireplace. As she peered down at the rough surface, she caught sight of tiny shards of black plastic.

"What is it, Nikki? What do you see?" Sonia leaned closer and tried to see over her shoulder.

"It's plastic." Nikki picked up a piece between her fingernails. "Just like the plastic that was found out in the snow the night that Ashley was killed."

"Are you sure? It's such tiny fragments, it could be from anything." Sonia took a slight step back.

"It could be. But it's quite a coincidence to find the same color plastic here. Where do you think it came from?" Nikki looked up at her. "Do you remember Kyle putting his boots up here?"

"No." Sonia cleared her throat and glanced away.

"We haven't either. We always leave ours by the door. Maybe one of the dogs tracked it in?" Nikki grabbed a piece of paper and began to gather the other pieces of plastic onto it.

"No, I don't think it was one of the dogs." Sonia sank down onto the edge of the couch and sighed.

"Sonia?" Nikki turned towards her. "Are you okay?"

"Ken had his boots propped up there, the whole time he was here." Sonia closed her eyes. "It must have come off his boots. I hate to think it, but I don't know how else it would have gotten there."

"There are a few ways I'm sure." Nikki frowned as she sat down beside her. "I don't want to think it either, but I suspected the plastic at the crime scene might be from sunglasses or ski goggles. I thought about it because I saw Brent buy sunglasses at the gas station we stopped at on our way here. I thought it was strange, because who needs sunglasses in the middle of a snowstorm?"

"Maybe Brent bought them for the snow. The glare off the snow can be quite strong." Sonia shrugged. "I've seen a lot of people on the slopes with sunglasses."

"Yes, you're right that's possible."

"Ken mentioned he had to buy ski goggles, remember?" Nikki began to pace.

"I do."

"What possible motive could Brent or Ken have? Would Ashley going through Brent's stuff and letting herself into Ken's cabin really be enough reason for either of them to kill her?"

"I don't think so. I haven't really spent time with Brent, but he seems nice enough, and Ken seems like a pretty even-tempered guy." Sonia picked up the used wine glasses and carried them into the kitchenette.

"Anyone can seem even-tempered with a glass of wine and a little effort." Nikki joined her near the sink. "But that doesn't mean he doesn't have another side."

"I'm not saying he doesn't." Sonia turned to face her. "I just think before we jump to conclusions, we need to be sure. Without a stronger motive, I can't see him as the killer."

"We need to know more about Ken. But I don't even know his last name, do you?" Nikki frowned.

"Actually no, he didn't mention it." Sonia turned the tap on and watched as the water splashed into the wine glasses. "In fact, he avoided anything too personal while we talked. He said he didn't have anyone to spend Christmas with."

"Can you believe that Christmas is only two days away?" Nikki winced. "I'm sorry, I know this isn't how you planned to spend the holiday."

"It's not your fault, Nikki." Sonia turned off the tap and took her hand. "I'm glad I'm here with you. None of us planned for this to happen, that's for sure."

"No, we didn't." Nikki's mind flickered with thoughts of her parents. How would they feel if they showed up for Christmas to find out that Kyle was behind bars? She didn't want them to go through that. She narrowed her eyes. "We have to solve this, Sonia. This isn't how we're going to spend the holidays."

"What do you have in mind?" Sonia raised an eyebrow.

"Something Quinn said to me. He said, the answer is in the evidence. I've already gone over the evidence from the crime scene, and it hasn't really led us anywhere. But what about the pictures that Ashley took? Maybe she was trying to leave a message, or at the very least gather evidence." Nikki walked over to the counter and picked up the camera.

"If only we could get in her head for a few minutes, have an idea as to why she thought these particular items were important enough to photograph, we might be able to get somewhere." Sonia joined her at the table. "But I just can't picture what she might have been thinking."

"Me either." Nikki sighed as she began to flip through the pictures. "Blonde hair bleach."

"None of our suspects have blonde hair. Betsy and Max have dark hair, Gloria has red hair, Brent has black hair and Ken's is light brown." Sonia shook her head. "I don't see how the hair bleach can help."

"Maybe we can look up the brand of wine." Nikki looked up at Sonia. "Maybe it's unique enough to give us some kind of clue about why she took the picture. We can also track the location of the toll booth from the receipt. Maybe that will connect to the wine somehow." Nikki sighed and sat back against the couch. "It's a stretch, but it could lead to something."

"It looks like the wine is only sold at one winery, it is also the vineyard where the wine is produced." Sonia scrolled through the website of the winery. "There's a contact number, but I'm not sure that would help us much. The winery is in Ettowah, it's a small town about thirty miles north of here."

"North?" Nikki tipped her head to the side. "Interesting. The toll booth is located to the north as well, let's see how far apart they are." She typed in the names of the two towns and looked over the map generated. "Only about fifteen miles apart." She tapped her fingertips lightly on the table. "I think we can assume that these two items belonged to the same person."

"Which might mean that the blonde hair bleach probably belonged to that person as well." Sonia sighed. "Unfortunately, that doesn't tell us who the person is."

"No, it doesn't." Nikki frowned. "But some toll booths have cameras. If this person took the time to get a receipt, we might be able to see who it is on camera."

"How are we going to get access to the cameras, though?" Sonia looked across the table at her.

"Luckily, I have a friend in the police department." Nikki cast a wink in her direction.

"A friend?" Sonia smiled. "I think perhaps he's a little more than that."

Nikki rolled her eyes as she put her phone to her ear. Seconds later she smiled at the sound of Quinn's voice.

"Hi Nikki, how's the weather looking up there? I hear you're getting more snow."

"Nothing but snow." Nikki sighed. "It would be a beautiful, white Christmas if I could think about anything other than murderers."

"Still no progress on the murder? Is Kyle doing okay?"

"He's fine. So far." Nikki winced as she recalled their last conversation. "Quinn, I'm worried the cops here aren't really doing a thorough enough investigation. I know it's a lot to ask, but I was hoping you might be able to do me a favor?"

"Sure, what do you need?"

"I have a toll receipt. I think it might be connected with the killer, but honestly we're not sure yet. I'd just like to know if there's a camera at this toll booth, and if so, can you take a look at who might have passed through the toll at the time of the receipt?" Nikki held her breath as she knew it was more than just a small favor.

"I can do that, Nikki. It will take a little time.

Send me a picture of the receipt, I can get all of the information I need off that."

"Thanks Quinn." Nikki sighed with relief.

"Anything at all, Nikki. Just send it to me. I'll get the information to you as soon as I can." Quinn paused, then spoke up again. "Nikki, call me later if you have some time to talk. All right?"

"Sure, is everything okay?" Her heart skipped a beat as she wondered if she'd asked for too much.

"I'd just like some time to talk with you, that's all. I'll get back to you on this as soon as I can." Quinn hung up the phone.

Fear jolted through Nikki. He just wanted to talk? What if he wanted to talk because he'd decided that she wasn't as interesting as he first thought? What if he wanted to put the brakes on a relationship that hadn't even gotten started? She stared at the phone for a moment.

"Is he going to help?" Sonia leaned across the table to meet her eyes.

"Yes, he's going to help." Nikki pushed thoughts of Quinn from her mind. She couldn't be distracted by them at the moment. "Okay, so pretty soon we should hopefully know who went through that toll booth. It's pretty clear that Ashley was playing detective, so my guess is she suspected this person of something."

"Maybe she was on to something?" Sonia stood up and walked over to the couch, where Princess was curled up.

"We know that she went to a lot of trouble to hide this camera, and since these are the only three pictures on the camera, and there was no dust on the statue, that means that she probably took them very recently." Nikki walked over to the couch and sat down beside her. "We know that she had many arguments with Max and Gloria, she had a run-in with Brent, and she went into Ken's cabin against his wishes. The only one that doesn't seem to have a motive is Betsy, but what was her scarf doing near the body. Did Betsy really give the scarf to Ashley as a gift?"

"Maybe Ken had something to hide?" Sonia stroked Princess' fur. "Maybe that's why he didn't want her in there. It could be that he is just a very private person, though."

"Let's say that's all that it is." Nikki shrugged and reached over to pet Princess as well. "The more important question is, why did Ashley go into his cabin without his permission? Presuming that Brent is telling the truth and she did go in. Something had to drive her to do that. Was it just an obsession with cleanliness, or was it something more?"

"What could it be?" Sonia shook her head. "That's the problem. We have no idea who he is or where he comes from."

"Which in itself, is a little unusual, isn't it?" Nikki narrowed her eyes. "He's made it pretty clear that he's interested in you, so why hasn't he told you anything serious about himself? It seems like he's probably used to hiding things."

"That may be, but again, we can't know it for sure." Sonia frowned. "I'll admit, I'm hoping it's not the case that he's involved."

"I can tell you that Max certainly has the temperament to kill Ashley, and he had a far stronger motive. I'm just not sure how any of this evidence could connect to him." Nikki set the camera down, then looked towards the window. "I've been in his home, but I haven't been in the second cabin where his dogs live. I bet if he has any secrets, that is where he would keep them. I am going to see if I can take a look."

"I'll go with you." Sonia started to stand up.

"No, I need you to stay here, and chat Ken up a bit. Maybe find out his last name, or at least an idea of where he comes from." Nikki walked over to her coat and began to pull it on. "Sonia, all I'm going to do is take a peek, I'm not going to go in. I'll get an idea of whether we can get inside, and I'll report back to you."

"Promise?" Sonia walked her to the door.

"I promise." Nikki leaned over and gave her a quick hug.

CHAPTER 14

The snow began to fall harder as Nikki walked past the lobby. She could hear the sound of the dogs barking. It saved her the trouble of trying to find out where Max's other cabin was located. Their barks carried across the wide, white fields. The new snowfall made her uneasy as she was aware that it would hamper the attempts at clearing the roads. Luckily, it was fairly light. She neared the cabin where she could hear the dogs barking. Before she could get to it, she noticed a police snowmobile parked in front of it. Officer Conner stood at the door of the cabin, with Max in front of him. Nikki drew back against the corner of another cabin, and watched as the two interacted.

"I need a good accounting of where Ashley was

that day. Otherwise, we can't narrow down who might have had contact with her. So, if you know something, you need to tell me." Conner stepped closer to Max. "Do you want this all to fall on your wife's shoulders? Because that's where it's headed."

"What about the boy, Kyle?" Max's voice wavered with frustration. "I thought you were honing in on him."

"We are, but his motive is weak. So, he had a few run-ins with Ashley, and they might have fought. He has no history of violent or criminal behavior. As it stands, he's our best suspect, but we'd like to clear everyone else that had regular contact with Ashley. I can't do that if I have no idea where she was the day she was killed." Conner shrugged, glanced over his shoulder as if he might have heard something, then looked back at Max. "Anything you can tell me would be helpful."

Nikki held her breath as she wondered if she'd been heard. She willed herself not to shift her feet in the crunchy snow again. Her stomach churned with fear as Conner's words replayed through her mind. Kyle was their best suspect? Shock bolted through her as she realized her brother might really be arrested for something he had nothing to do with. Once he was handcuffed there would be nothing that she could do to stop it. He would be at the mercy of the courts.

"All right, well, I know she took out one of the snowmobiles. I was going to write her up, because she brought it back with some damage to it. They're all equipped with GPS trackers, so there's a record of where she went and when. I checked it, and the log said she took a trip up Fir Mountain. That area is out of bounds at the moment. I have no idea what she might have been doing up there." Max shooed the dogs back from the officer. "Will that help?"

"That will help a lot. Where are the snowmobiles?" Conner pulled out his notepad.

"The garage is right behind the main lobby. If you ask Gloria, she'll give you a pass to get in. You're welcome to look at anything you want." Max sighed and lowered his voice. "Just go easy on Gloria, she's a sensitive person. She's harmless, but she barks louder than my girls." He gave Marshmallow a solid pat on the side.

"Thanks for the tip." Conner tucked his notepad back into his pocket. "I'll be in touch."

"That reminds me. It seems one of our passes is missing, it unlocks all of the cabins. I haven't been able to find it. We thought maybe Ashley had it on her person when she died. Do you have any record of that?" Max locked eyes with the officer.

Nikki's heart skipped a beat. That pass was tucked away in her purse.

"No, there's no record of her having it on her at the time. Do you have any idea who else might have taken it?" Conner's voice elevated with interest.

"No, but I can deactivate it. I can also check where it was used last, and when. A record is made every time it's used." Max frowned. "My guess is only the employees would have access."

"Thanks. Please let me know when you have that information ready." Conner walked back towards the snowmobile.

Nikki ducked around the corner of the cabin and took a sharp breath. She realized that if they checked the records, they would see that it had been used to go into Ashley's cabin after she had died. If they believed an employee had stolen it, their first suspicions would fall on Kyle. She winced at the knowledge that her actions had likely made the case against Kyle even stronger. It seemed every step she attempted to take to protect her brother ended up backfiring. But there was one good thing. She knew that she could find out where Ashley had been on the day of her death. If the snowmobile had a record of where she went, then she could travel to the same place on Fir Mountain. Clearly there was something on Fir Mountain. She could only hope that it would be enough to clear her brother's name and incriminate the actual murderer.

Once Nikki was sure that Max had gone inside, and Conner had taken off on the snowmobile, she headed back towards her cabin. There was no way that she could get anywhere near Max's cabin without setting the dogs off, and even if she could, the pass wouldn't work anymore. Maybe she couldn't get to any of Max's secrets, but she could still figure out Ashley's. She recalled her promise to Kyle. No, it wasn't wise to think about going to Fir Mountain on her own, but she would do anything to protect her brother. When she arrived at the cabin, Sonia greeted her at the door.

"How did it go?" Her wide, anxious eyes searched Nikki's.

"They are definitely focusing in on Kyle. And this keycard is useless now." Nikki pulled it out of her purse and tossed it into the trashcan. As she filled her in about Ashley's trip to Fir Mountain, she crouched down to pet Coco. "Hey buddy, how are you?" She smiled as he licked her cheeks.

"What was she up to?" Sonia shook her head.

"Honestly, it almost feels as if she was trying to blackmail someone. But what could wine, a toll receipt, and some hair bleach have to do with incriminating someone?"

"I don't know." Nikki shook her head. "What's that?" She tipped her head towards a grocery bag on the counter.

"Ken brought us some more food. He went out for a trip on his snowmobile to the nearest store before the snow gets too heavy again. Also, I found out his last name." Sonia smiled as she met Nikki's eyes. "It's Berjen."

"Berjen?" Nikki snapped her fingers. "Good, now maybe we can find out some information about him." As she dug through the bag of groceries, she found a bottle of wine, a bag of grapes, and some cheese. "He knows his way around a cheese plate, hmm?" Nikki smiled.

"I hope you don't mind, but I invited him over for tomorrow night. Since, it's Christmas Eve." Sonia grabbed the bottle of wine and tucked it into the small refrigerator. "We'll just let this chill until then."

"That's right, I forgot it's almost Christmas Eve." Nikki's heart sank as she checked her phone for any texts from her parents. "What a terrible holiday this is going to be."

"Don't give up hope yet, Nikki. This is the time of year when miracles happen, right?" Sonia gave her a light pat on the cheek. "Don't lose that optimism, dear."

"You're right." Nikki took a deep breath. "Maybe Quinn can dig up something on Ken." She sent a text to Quinn with Ken's name. Then she fired off a text to Kyle about the developments in the case.

When he texted back, his words were firm.

Stay off Fir Mountain.

Nikki's fingers trembled as she typed back a promise that she would. She knew that it was a promise she couldn't keep.

In the darkness just before dawn, Nikki made her plan. It hinged on getting out of the cabin before Sonia woke up. If she woke up, she knew there was no way that she would let her leave alone. She also knew that there was no way she could let Sonia be in danger.

As soon as she saw the faintest light peek through the curtains she climbed out of bed. She pulled on two layers of thick socks. Then two layers of sweatpants. She layered a long-sleeve shirt and a sweatshirt. By the time she was done she was already sweating, but she knew that she would be thankful for the warmth later. She slid a thick pair of gloves over a thin pair of gloves. Finally, she donned her scarf, and a coat. She felt about thirty pounds heavier, but she hoped all of the layers would protect her from the icy wind. As she stepped out the door, her heart began to pound. She had no idea what she was about to get herself into, but she knew there was nothing safe about it.

"And just where do you think you're going?" Kyle looked over at her as she pushed the door closed behind her.

"Shh, I don't want you to wake Sonia." Nikki frowned as she realized she had been caught.

"I still can't get used to you calling her that." Kyle grinned, then his expression grew more serious. He straightened up and turned to face her. "Where are you going?"

"Kyle, I just want to see if there's something up there to find. Now I know Ashley was up there. She used one of the snowmobiles from the resort to get there. Which means she probably planned to meet someone. With the GPS record on the snowmobile, I can find the exact spot she traveled to." She crossed her arms as she studied him. "I'm going to be careful."

"It's way too dangerous. Why don't you understand that?" Kyle spread his feet apart as he blocked her way. "I'm not letting you go."

"Kyle, you can't stop me." Nikki attempted to step around him.

"I can, and I will." He moved in front of her before she could get past.

"Kyle! Please, I need to work out who did this, before it's too late and you land up in jail." Nikki glared at him.

"I hate it when you're right." He rubbed his hand across the thick hat he wore and frowned.

"You should be used to it by now." Nikki raised an eyebrow.

"Very funny." Kyle sighed, looked towards the mountains, then turned his attention back to her. "I'll go with you, but the moment I see anything that looks dangerous, we're out of there. Agreed?"

"Agreed." Nikki smiled and elbowed him in the side. "I knew you would come around."

"Careful, I can still push you down in the snow, and I'm pretty sure in that outfit, you're not going to be able to get back up." Kyle quirked an eyebrow.

"Don't you dare!" Nikki scowled at him.

"It worked when you were ten." He grinned.

"This is serious, Kyle, we're only going to get one chance at this." Nikki met his eyes. "Mom and Dad are going to be here tomorrow, they sent me their flight confirmation. I don't want them to come here to find out that I wasn't able to keep you safe."

"And what if they come here and find out that I didn't keep you safe?" Kyle stared straight back at her. "We're in this together, sis, no matter what."

"Yes, we are. First things first, we've got to get our hands on that snowmobile." Nikki frowned as she started towards the main lobby.

"That won't be a problem." Kyle pulled a set of keys from his pocket. "I have access to the snowmobiles. Do you know which one it was?"

"Yes, because it's due for repairs. Just for some body damage. Ashley must have clipped something." Nikki tipped her head towards the lobby. "Do you think we can get it out of there without anyone noticing?"

"It shouldn't be a problem." Kyle looked at his watch. "The water pump turns on in a few minutes.

We'll take it out then. The noise will mask the sound of the engine." He smiled. "Sound good?"

"How did you get to be such a criminal mastermind?" Nikki smiled.

"I had to sneak out of the house somehow." Kyle winked at her, then led the way towards the garage behind the lobby. A quick swipe of his pass allowed the garage door to slide open. Nikki ducked under it and slipped inside while it was still ascending. A sea of snowmobiles and other equipment made her dizzy for a moment. Could she find the right one? One by one she checked each snowmobile for damage.

"Here it is!" Nikki slapped the seat and glanced over at Kyle.

"I'll drive." He hopped on and she climbed on behind him. He brought up the last location on the GPS. "Ready?"

"Yes." Nikki hung on to the sides.

As the water pump started Kyle started up the engine.

It occurred to Nikki as she gripped the handles, that she had never actually been on a snowmobile.

CHAPTER 15

ikki ignored a rush of nerves as Kyle drove out through the front door of the shed. He veered off to the left, away from the lobby windows. The snowmobile cut through the snow with speed that surprised Nikki. She tightened her grip and leaned her head down as snow flew towards her face. As he emerged from the trail, he skidded to a stop.

"Great." Nikki sighed as she met his eyes. "The hard part is over."

"No, sis, that wasn't the hard part." Kyle pulled his goggles down over his eyes, then zipped his jacket up so that the stiff collar shielded his mouth.

Nikki followed suit. It crossed her mind that maybe they should turn back, but she bit back her words. It was too late to turn back, and she felt this was the best way to keep Kyle out of jail. As they whirred past the cabins decorated with sparkling lights and garland for Christmas, she realized that it was Christmas Eve. She hadn't even thought about the holiday with everything that was going on. She wanted more than anything to be spending the holiday around a fire with her family and friends close to her. Instead, her brother and her were going up the side of a dangerous mountain. He pulled off to the side of a particularly steep trail, and turned to her.

"It gets treacherous from here." Kyle looked at the GPS. "It's not far, ten more minutes up I think."

"Good." Nikki nodded.

"But we can't go this way." Kyle tipped his head towards the trail. "See how loose the snow is? That's from a recent slide, we could get stuck in it."

"That way?" Nikki pointed to a trail that veered off to the right.

"I've never been on it before." Kyle frowned. "We need to take it slow. I don't want to get stranded up here." He eased along. "Only a few minutes ahead, Nikki!" Kyle glided in the direction the GPS showed him. A few minutes later, he pulled into a clearing. On one side was a wide-open slope of snow, on the other was the solid rock face of the mountain. Nikki climbed off the snowmobile and stared at the mostly empty surroundings. Only one tree rose up out of the snow, and it was fairly small.

"Fir Mountain." Kyle looked over at her. "I brought you here, even though I know how dangerous it is, and there's nothing here."

"There has to be." Nikki frowned. "I know it. Maybe she hid something here."

"Where?" Kyle gestured to the snow all around them. "There aren't exactly a ton of hiding places."

"She would have put it somewhere that would be easy to get to, and easy to remember." Nikki started towards the tree. "There!" She pointed to a crook in the tree that was piled with snow. Its other branches only had a small amount of snow on them, but it looked to her that someone had packed snow into the crook between two branches.

"Let me take a look." Kyle began to brush the snow away.

"Is there something there?" Nikki leaned close to him in an attempt to see what he uncovered.

"Yes, there's something." Kyle pulled a small, metal box, the size of a postcard, and about six inches deep, out of the snow. "But it's locked." He frowned as he looked up at her. "The lock seems pretty solid."

"So, she went to all the trouble of taking this up the side of a mountain, hiding it in the snow, and locking it up tight. There must be something very important inside." Nikki took the box from him. "Do you think we can break it open somehow?"

"I don't have any tools with me. I think we're better off heading back, we can pry it open when we get there." Kyle glanced up at the mountain above him. "I don't like the way that pile of snow above us looks. We need to get going."

"Okay, let's head back." Nikki climbed on the snowmobile behind him and tucked the box into her coat pocket. As he started the engine, she heard a strange roar. She glanced over at Kyle, just as he jumped off the snowmobile and lunged in her direction.

"Nikki!" Kyle shouted her name as the roar got louder. When his body collided with hers and knocked her off the snowmobile, she didn't know what was happening, but she knew that it was bad. He pulled her up to her feet. "Run!" He hung onto her arm as he half-dragged her towards the moun-tain. Finally, she realized that a wall of snow had begun to slide down the side of the mountain. She gasped as it dawned on her that there was nowhere to run. Kyle thrust her ahead of him towards the mountain. Only then did she realize that there was a slim opening. He wedged himself in behind her, just as the wall of snow crashed down along the side of the mountain. Within seconds the opening of the tiny cave was completely blocked by snow.

"Kyle!" Nikki gasped again as snow spilled into the cave.

"It's all right." Kyle wrapped his arms around her. "The snow will pack down before it can fill the cave. It's going to block us in, but it won't get much farther into the cave."

"I can't believe it!" Nikki stared at the wall of snow. She'd never seen anything like it before.

"I warned you that it wasn't safe up here." Kyle pulled her farther back against the inside of the cave. "We could be buried alive right now."

"I'm sorry, Kyle." Nikki clung to his hand as she peered at the heavily packed snow. "Is there any way for us to get out of here?"

"Don't worry. You told Mrs. Whitter that we were coming up here right? She at least knows that was your plan?" Kyle shrugged. "I'm sure she'll sound the alarm if she doesn't hear from us."

"Actually." Nikki winced as she looked at him. "I

didn't tell her. I knew that if I did, she would want to come with me. I couldn't take a chance that she could be hurt. That something like this could happen." She blinked back tears. "That's why I didn't want to wake her this morning."

"I thought you just didn't want to because it was too early." Kyle groaned. "Nikki. It's an important rule, if you're going to go out onto the mountains, you always let someone know where you're going. Are you telling me no one knows we're here?"

"I'm sorry." Nikki took a deep breath. "But try not to worry, we're going to find our way out." She willed herself to be strong and have a positive attitude for her brother, even if pure panic had begun to build up within her.

"How?" Kyle threw his hands up into the air. "How do you think we're going to get out?"

"Maybe we can call—" Nikki cut herself off as she realized how ridiculous that was. Of course there wouldn't be any service. She checked her phone just to be sure.

"Nikki, nothing is going to get through that snow." Kyle walked over to the snow and began to dig into it. "Even if we were able to get through it, there is a ton of snow piled on top of it, it would only make it start sliding again."

"What are you saying, Kyle?" Nikki's eyes widened as she stared at him. "Are you saying we're never going to get out of here?"

"I'm saying." Kyle took a breath as he met her eyes. "I'm saying that it could take a while before anyone notices that we're missing. We don't have any food, or water, and it's going to get colder and colder. I'm sorry, Nikki, I'd like to tell you that everything is going to be fine, but it's not."

"I did this." Nikki sank down to her knees as the weight of their situation struck her. "I made us come up here. I wanted to protect you, but all I've done is put you in the worst possible situation."

"Nikki." Kyle crouched down in front of her and put his hands on her shoulders. "It's not your fault. I chose to come with you. I knew the risks, better than you ever could. I should have stopped you."

"What are we going to do, Kyle?" Nikki bit into her bottom lip in an attempt to keep her chin from trembling.

"Let's look around." Kyle turned on the flashlight on his phone. "Maybe there's something in here that can help."

"I'll look, too." Nikki turned the flashlight on her phone on as well. A sinking sensation threatened to knock her back to her knees as she realized that the battery would only last so long. Then they would be surrounded by darkness. The cave was barely big enough for both of them to sit in comfortably. There was nothing on the stone floor or walls that would help in their situation. She began to dig through her purse, but knew there wouldn't be much there that could help either. When she started going through her pockets her fingers bumped into the small, metal box.

"Kyle! Maybe we could use the box to carve out a tunnel in the snow? I know you said it will keep sliding, but it's worth a try isn't it?" Nikki pulled out the box to show him.

"The only way it will work is if the slide was contained mostly to the side of the mountain. If we're able to get a hole through it, then we might be able to get out." Kyle frowned. "But it's risky." He took the box from her. "It's our only shot, though." He slammed the metal box against the ground.

"Kyle! What are you doing?" Nikki gasped as the box clanged against the stone.

"It'll work better if it's empty." Kyle picked up the box again and slammed it back down against the ground. "You can't pick a lock, can you?"

"No." Nikki frowned. "Here, try this." She

grabbed a piece of rock. "It might break the lock free."

"Thanks, I'll give it a shot." Kyle slammed the rock down against the lock. A second later the lid of the box popped open.

CHAPTER 16

Sonia jerked awake. Her heart raced. She had no idea why, until she heard the dogs barking. Both dogs were at the door of the cabin, and both barked so loudly that she had to cover her ears.

"What is it? Nikki? What's going on?" Sonia got to her feet and called to the dogs. "Enough, quiet!"

The dogs quietened down, but still whimpered near the door. Sonia noticed that there was no sign of Nikki in the cabin. She discovered a note on the kitchen counter.

Gone out for a bit, will be back soon.

Sonia narrowed her eyes as she read over the note again. It couldn't be more vague. Where had she gone, and when? It only took her a few minutes to figure it out. Nikki had gone to Fir Mountain. She was sure of it. But she had no idea when she had left. The clock on the wall declared it was already a little after nine. Sonia took out the dogs, then started the coffee pot as her heart continued to pound. If she had gone up the mountain, what if something had happened to her? She gritted her teeth as she realized that Nikki had been careful not to wake her up, or mention her plans to her. Which meant she'd planned to do this without Sonia's involvement. As an hour slipped by, her worry increased.

Sonia gazed out the window as snow continued to fall. There was a time when she considered it beautiful, but now it was really getting old. The more snow that fell, the less chance there was of the roads being opened.

"Where are you, Nikki?" Sonia frowned. She tried her cell phone, and again was sent straight to voicemail. Either Nikki had turned her phone off, or she had no service, or something worse. She shuddered at the thought. "No, she's fine. I'm sure she's fine." She began to pace back and forth. She placed a call to Kyle. His phone also went to voicemail. Desperate, she decided to send a text to Quinn. She knew that Nikki wouldn't be happy when she found out, but Quinn was the only person she trusted to help. She placed a call to the local police as well. After that, she tried to reassure herself that everything would be fine. But with each snowflake that fell, her stomach twisted. Coco was dying for a walk. Nikki would know that. She would also know that Sonia couldn't handle walking both of the dogs for longer than it took for them to take a break. So why wasn't she back?

Sonia wrung her hands and continued to pace. A sharp knock on the door made her jump. She turned towards it. Maybe Nikki had forgotten her key? As she pulled open the door, she smiled in anticipation of seeing her friend. Instead Ken peered in at her.

"Weather turned. I just wanted to make sure you were okay over here." He stepped into the cabin.

"I can't talk now, Ken. Nikki is missing. I need to find out what's happened to her." Sonia pulled her phone out of her pocket. Maybe the police had found something, maybe Quinn had.

"Missing?" Ken took a step towards her. "You have no idea where she went?"

"Maybe I have some idea." She took a sharp breath, then met his eyes. "Can you take me somewhere on a snowmobile, Ken?"

"Of course, I can." He smiled. "Where do you want to go?"

"Fir Mountain." Sonia narrowed her eyes. "I'm sure that's where she went. I'm really worried about her. I think she might have gone off by herself. What if she's hurt?"

"Try not to worry." Ken reached for her hand. "Nikki is a big girl, she can handle herself."

"You don't understand, she'll do anything to protect her brother. What if she's taken things too far? I need to call and check with the police again." Sonia started to call.

"You won't be needing that." Ken snatched the phone out of her hand.

Coco leaped to his feet and began to bark at Ken.

"Quiet him, now, or we're going to have a problem." Ken remained in front of the door as he pocketed Sonia's phone.

"Shh, Coco." Sonia crouched down and ran her hand along the dog's fur. "It's all right." She gulped down the fear that flooded her as she looked in Ken's direction. It was clear to her that everything was not all right. Nikki had been right, Ken was a dangerous man.

"Good, go on, sit down." Ken gestured to the

couch. "I'm not going to hurt you, Sonia. Not if you don't give me a reason to."

"Ken. Why are you doing this?" Sonia watched as he headed for the kitchenette. She was tempted to jump up and run for the door, but she knew that he could beat her there.

"Where is that wine I brought you?" Ken rummaged through the kitchen.

"It's chilling." Sonia bit into her bottom lip to hold back a gasp.

"Great. Perfect." Ken pulled the bottle of wine out and smiled as he gazed at the label. "It's my favorite."

Sonia's eyes widened as she recognized the label. She hadn't really looked at it the night before. It was the same brand as the bottle of wine in the picture on Ashley's camera.

"It was you," Sonia whispered.

"Me?" Ken's eyes snapped towards her. "What do you know about me?"

"Nothing." Sonia cleared her throat. "I don't know anything, Ken. I wanted to know you. I thought you were a good man."

"I am." Ken opened the wine, then gathered two wine glasses. "Some would say I'm a very good man. I've been very generous throughout my life. But I

CINDY BELL

made one mistake." He filled both glasses to the brim, then set the bottle of wine down. "I took some things." He picked up the wine glasses and walked towards her. "And due to unfortunate circumstances, I had to kill someone to protect my identity, to keep from getting caught." He paused in front of her, and offered her one of the glasses. "Things get out of hand so quickly."

"No, thank you." Sonia drew back against the couch.

"Don't, don't do that." Ken squinted at her and thrust the glass towards her. A few drops of the liquid splashed over the brim of the glass and dropped down onto the white trousers he wore.

"I'm sorry," Sonia whispered, and took the glass from him.

"That's better. This doesn't have to be any different than we planned. Remember? We were going to spend the afternoon together." Ken sat down beside her. After a long swallow of his wine, he looked over at her. "You're such a wonderful woman, Sonia."

"What have you done to Nikki?" Sonia shivered as he leaned closer to her.

"What makes you think I've done anything to her?" Ken chuckled. "She was foolish enough to get herself in some bad circumstances. Nothing I can do about that."

"What circumstances?" Her heartbeat quickened, though it was already racing.

"Never mind that. I need to work out what to do with you, now that you know I am on the run."

"On the run?" Sonia stared at him, stunned by the revelation. She realized that Ken thought she knew many secrets about him.

Nikki gazed down into the open box. Her heart pounded as she saw the stack of photographs and papers. She reached into the box and pulled them out.

"This is what Ashley was hiding." Nikki pulled off one of her gloves and began to sift through the photographs. Max was featured prominently in the first few. There was a photograph of him with his two dogs, as well as one of him with Gloria. The third one showed Max, Gloria, and Ken huddled around the desk in the lobby. Beneath those, were more pictures. These featured Ken. Ken on the snowmobile, Ken with a bottle of wine in his hand, Ken putting on a pair of ski goggles.

"I don't understand, why are there so many pictures of Ken?" Nikki frowned as she dug a little deeper into the stack.

"Never mind that, give me the box." Kyle snatched it from her hands, then began to dig at the snow that blocked the door of the cave.

"Wait a minute." Nikki's eyes widened as she studied the pictures of Ken. One featured a birthmark on the back of his neck. Another depicted a scar on the back of his hand. "It's almost as if she was trying to identify him." She skimmed back over the other photographs. Suddenly her heart lurched. "It's the same wine in the photograph on Ashley's camera." She searched further and found a folded-up piece of paper. She opened it to reveal what looked like an article printed out from an online newspaper. *Wine Thief on the Run.* Nikki read through the article that detailed how a wine maker that used to work at a winery in Ettowah had taken off with thousands of dollars from takings and many bottles of wine, including a dozen vintage bottles of wine worth thousands. The thief was still on the run.

"Nikki, I don't think you know how serious our situation is here." Kyle shot her a stern look. "We need to get out of here."

"Yes, we do. Kyle, it was Ken. He's the one that killed Ashley, I know it. She was blackmailing him, that's why she wanted to meet him up here." Nikki frowned. "It's why he killed her. To keep his secret."

"Maybe, but if that's the case, then his problem is already solved. No one else knows what he's hiding." Kyle hacked at the snow in front of him. "And there's no way we are going to be able to tell them."

"Let me help." Nikki pulled one of her boots off and used the tread on the bottom to dig at the snow. By the time she finally dropped it, her arm felt as if it might fall off. She gazed at the minimal progress she had made. Kyle had managed to get through a bit of the snow, but the news wasn't good.

"The snow is thicker than I'd hoped. It's going to take some more time. We should rest for a few minutes." Kyle looked at her. "Nikki, we need to conserve as much energy and heat as we can. You need to turn off your flashlight, we'll just use mine."

As Nikki slid her finger across the screen to turn off her flashlight, she noticed the time. Stunned, she looked up at her brother.

"Merry Christmas, Kyle!"

"You're not serious?" He stepped closer to her. "Has it been that long?"

"I'm afraid so." Her chest tightened as she realized what that meant. There was a good chance that they wouldn't make it through the night, and just about zero chance that anyone was coming for them. It was so dark she shivered.

"It's Christmas." Kyle sighed and closed his eyes. "And we're stuck here. Mom and Dad are probably stranded at some airport. All because I had the good idea to invite you all here."

"Kyle, none of this is your fault." Nikki wrapped her arm around his shoulders. "You couldn't have known what was going to happen." She pulled him closer. "We just need to keep each other warm, and trust that someone will find us."

"It's hard for me to trust in something that's so unlikely." He frowned.

"What other choice do we have?" Nikki shivered as the cold seeped into her. The thought of the darkness that would surround them when they ran out of battery terrified her. But she needed to remain strong for Kyle. "We have to trust."

"You're right." Kyle rested his head back against the wall of the cave. "This is just some terrible set of circumstances. Maybe everything will turn around, maybe luck will be on our side. We need a miracle."

Nikki's stomach twisted as it occurred to her

that it might not have just been bad luck. If Ken was trying to hide something about himself, maybe he began to get suspicious of Sonia for asking questions. Maybe, he had decided that they were onto him. Maybe, he had followed them up the side of Fir Mountain.

"Kyle, what if we weren't alone up here?" Nikki tipped her head to the side to look at him. "What if someone trapped us in here?"

"I told you, it's dangerous up here. It's just a coincidence, Nikki. There is no way anyone could have caused this to happen." Kyle pulled away from her. "I'm going to see if I can dig a little more. You should try to get some rest."

"Kyle, you've barely sat down." Nikki grabbed his hand. "You're going to exhaust yourself."

"What does it matter?" Kyle glanced back at her. "If we don't get out of here, we're never going home, Nikki. Never."

Nikki realized that her brother had given up. She watched as he tore at the snow. Why wouldn't he give up? Things were stacked against them. Sonia's words carried through her mind. She'd encouraged her to stay optimistic. If that was the only tool she had left, then that was the tool she would use.

"I'm not going to need rest in here. We're going to get out of here soon." Nikki grabbed her boot and began hacking at the snow again.

"Easy Nikki, don't hurt yourself." Kyle ground the metal box into the snow. "I think we're making some progress. But if you hear a crack or a creek, get back right away. Snow is extremely heavy, it can crush us if we get caught under it."

"I'll be careful." Nikki continued to dig right beside him. Maybe it wasn't the way she had imagined spending Christmas morning, but she was glad that Kyle was with her. She'd prefer that he'd be somewhere far away and safe, but as it was, at least they had each other.

CHAPTER 17

Sonia looked over at the clock. It was almost midnight. She closed her eyes as Ken walked past her, then back towards the door.

"I just want to spend some time with you before I go. The roads are clearing up and I have to leave before dawn." He turned back to look at her.

Coco whined at the front door. Princess nuzzled deeper into Sonia's lap.

"Please, let me take the dogs out. It's been hours, they need to use the bathroom. Let me just get some fresh air, and then I'll spend whatever time I can with you. Okay?" Sonia's voice wavered as she spoke. She did her best to ignore the fear that bubbled up within her. She guessed that soon he would kill her. She wanted to buy some time. Her thoughts remained on Nikki. She knew now that there was no chance Nikki was somewhere safe. She would never be gone so long.

"Fine, take the dogs out." Ken crossed his arms as he stared at her. "I'll be going with you. If you try to get anyone's attention, if you try to run, your time will be up." Ken locked his eyes to hers.

"I won't do any of that." Sonia shook her head. "I promise."

"Good." Ken smiled as he stroked her cheek. "I didn't think that you would, but I thought it would be best to make things clear."

"Crystal clear." Sonia managed a smile.

"Excellent. Make sure you bundle up. It's freezing out there." Ken gestured to her coat on the coat rack near the door.

"Sure." Sonia grabbed her coat, slid on her boots, and even wrapped a scarf around her neck. However, at the last moment she pulled the scarf back off. Wasn't that how Ashley had died? She didn't want to give Ken any ideas. It made her feel sick to think that she hadn't really suspected him. She was more eager to believe that the killer was Gloria, or Betsy, or Max, or Brent, than to even consider that it could be Ken. Now that she knew for sure, she still couldn't quite wrap her head around it. How could a man as fascinating and eloquent as Ken turn out to be one of the worst kinds of people, a murderer? As she put on Princess' leash, she felt her heart lurch. She needed to protect the dogs. She needed to keep them safe.

Sonia stepped out into the brisk night air, and realized it was colder than she had ever felt it. Ice seemed to flow through her veins as she held tightly to the leashes. If Nikki was there, she would know exactly what to do to keep the dogs calm. Especially since she was sure that they could both tell just how frightened she was. But even though she was scared Sonia knew that she would do anything to keep Princess and Coco safe.

Sonia was a few steps away from the door of the cabin, with Ken right behind her, when she heard sudden footsteps, and then a thump. She gasped and spun around in time to see a figure wrestling Ken to the ground.

Coco began to bark, and soon Princess joined in. Both dogs created quite a commotion, at a time when most guests at the resort would have been sleeping. As the man on top of Ken finally subdued him, Sonia heard the sound of handcuffs clicking shut.

"Quinn?" Sonia squinted through the darkness at the man who got to his feet.

"Sonia." Quinn met her eyes. "Are you okay? Did he hurt you?"

"No, he didn't hurt me. I'm fine." She shook her head as she stared at him. "What are you doing here? How did you know to come?"

"Where's Nikki?" Quinn looked back towards the cabin. "I've been watching through the window for a chance to get to Ken, but I didn't see her inside. I got your text earlier saying you weren't sure where she was. Is she still missing?"

"Yes, Quinn I'm sorry. It's been hours." Sonia gasped as Ken squirmed on the ground.

"Don't worry, he's not going anywhere." Quinn gestured to Conner and Schwitz who had been hidden by the side of the cabin. "We know exactly who you are." Quinn stared down at the man in handcuffs. "You're not getting away."

"What do you mean, Quinn?" Sonia took a step towards him. "We have to do something. Explain to me what you're talking about?"

"What's going on here?" Max jogged up to the scene.

"This man, who you know as Ken, is on the run for theft. I was able to link together the date from the toll receipt and the date of the theft. He worked for the winery in Ettowah and took off with thousands of dollars, and thousands of dollars worth of wine. After Nikki sent me the name he was using, I ran it through the system. It popped up as a potential alias, and I began to sort through the information that she had given me. The pictures she sent matched the information that was on file about him. Where the money was stolen from, the direction he would have been coming from, and the blonde hair bleach." He narrowed his eyes. "When I couldn't get in contact with either you or Nikki, my instincts told me that you were stuck here with a murderer."

"Wait, the hair bleach?" Sonia frowned. "Ken has light brown hair, not blonde."

"Actually, he has dark hair. Black." Quinn glanced over at Ken as he was escorted away. "In order to dye it light brown, he would have had to bleach it first, which explains the blonde hair bleach. I reached out to the local police department and found there had been a few tips called in about his possible presence in this area. That's when I decided I needed to get here." He shook his head as his gaze swept across the snow. "Luckily, the local police department was willing to assist me in getting through the roads. They're now participating in the investigation. Officer Conner and Schwitz have been helping me."

"Good, because I have some information to report to them. Someone has stolen a snowmobile from the garage. It was taken by Kyle." Max glared at Sonia. "But I can guess who he was with."

"Kyle is with her. I knew it." Sonia sighed with relief. "At least she is not alone."

"Is there any record of where the snowmobile went?" Quinn took a step towards Max. His eyes narrowed as they locked on Max.

"What are you going to do when you find them? I want to know that you are going to arrest them for theft." Max crossed his arms.

"Don't give me any trouble." Quinn crossed the small distance between them until he was nearly nose to nose with the man. "I know what you were doing. I know that you were trying to let Kyle take the fall to get the attention off you and your wife."

"All right, all right." Max took a step back and held up his hands. "I just needed to protect what was mine. Besides, how was I supposed to know that Kyle was innocent?"

"Just tell us where they went." Sonia's voice cut through the tension between the two men. "Tell us now, Max, that's all we care about. Everything else will be forgotten."

Quinn shot her a brief look, but didn't say anything to contradict her.

"Here." Max held out his phone to Sonia. "The GPS app is on and already set to the missing snowmobile. It shows their location earlier today. But the signal was lost a few hours ago. You can follow it up to the last place they were. It's very dangerous in that area at the moment." He lowered his voice. "If that's where they went, then it's probably already too late."

"What a terrible thing to say." Sonia swatted at him.

"Hey, watch it!" Max scowled as he backed away from her.

"Sonia, don't." Quinn caught her hand. "The important thing right now is that we find Nikki and Kyle."

"Yes, let's get going. Let me just get the dogs inside." Sonia started towards the door.

"No Sonia." Quinn met her eyes. "You aren't coming with me. You know that Nikki wouldn't want you to. I need you to stay here in case she finds her way back."

"Quinn, I—"

"The more you argue the longer they are sitting out there in the cold somewhere!" Quinn's voice sharpened, then he frowned. "I'm sorry, but I don't have time to debate." He looked at Max. "Can you bring your dogs to help look for them?"

"No way." Max shook his head. "There is no way I am going on that mountain, it is too dangerous."

"Can I take the dogs then?" Quinn narrowed his eyes.

"Sorry, but no, they won't listen to you."

"Okay." Quinn gritted his teeth, clearly furious. "I don't have time to argue. I will have to take Coco then." Quinn took Coco's leash from Sonia. "I'm going to find them both, Sonia, I promise."

Sonia winced as she watched him take off across the snow, with Coco in tow. She wanted more than anything to be at his side. But she knew he was right. Nikki had gone to a lot of trouble to make sure that she remained safe. As she carried Princess inside the cabin, her heart pounded. The killer had been caught, but that didn't mean that he hadn't already claimed the lives of two more victims. Nikki and Kyle had gone up the mountain to find the truth, she just hoped that they would be able to come back down again. She closed her eyes and leaned against the cabin door.

"Nikki, help is coming, sweetheart, just hang in there."

Nikki's eyes popped open. She shivered as she realized that she must have fallen asleep. She reached for her phone to check the time, and found that it wouldn't turn on. The battery was dead.

Kyle grunted as he slammed the box into the snow.

"Kyle, you have to take a break. Come sit with me and warm up." Nikki opened her arms to him as he slumped down to the ground beside her.

"I'm sorry, Nikki, I can't get through."

"It's all right." She patted his leg. "Everything's going to be fine."

"We're not getting out of here." Kyle shuddered. "It's impossible."

"We will. I know we will." She tilted her head

until she could look into his eyes. "It's Christmas, Kyle. Later today, we'll be sitting around a fire, with Mom and Dad, and all of this will be a memory."

"Are you kidding, Mom and Dad are going to kill us when they find out about this." Kyle managed a short laugh.

"Yes, well, they might. But then there will be a fire, and cookies. Lots of cookies." Nikki closed her eyes and thought she could taste them on the tip of her tongue. "There will be Christmas music, and we'll all be together, Kyle, just like we were supposed to be."

"I wish I could believe that." Kyle sighed.

"Believe it. With everything you have left in you. Believe it with me." Nikki started to say more, when she heard a sound that made her heart skip a beat.

"Nikki, I know you're trying—"

"Shh!" Nikki suddenly stood up and moved towards the front of the cave. "Do you hear that?"

"Hear what?" Kyle frowned as she started to dig at the snow. "Don't bother, Nikki, we can't get through."

"It's Coco!" Nikki gasped as she heard the familiar bark again. "Kyle, it's Coco!"

"Nikki, you're imagining things." Kyle shook his

head. Then suddenly he stood up. "I hear it, too! Hey!" He shouted at the wall of snow. "Hey! We're in here!"

"Do you think anyone can hear us?" Nikki met his eyes.

"I'm sure going to try to be heard." Kyle began to shout again.

"Help! We're here!" Nikki joined in on the shouting.

Coco's barking got closer. She couldn't tell exactly where he was, but she guessed that he had stopped, because his barking seemed to come from only one direction. She heard scratching.

"He's digging." Nikki's eyes filled with tears. "He's digging, Kyle, he's found us!"

"Good dog." Kyle laughed and blinked back his own tears. "Come on, Coco, we're in here."

"Good boy, Coco." Nikki dug at the snow from the inside.

"Coco, come away!" A muffled voice called out.

Coco barked, but the sound became distant.

"Oh no." Nikki's heart dropped. "Someone's taking him away."

"Hey!" Kyle pounded on the snow. "Come back!"

Seconds later, a loud engine whirred to life.

"They're going to get us out!" Kyle gasped as he looked at Nikki. "They've got the equipment to get us out."

Nikki threw her arms around Kyle and hugged him. As the snow began to crumble away from the opening of the cave, she felt relief more intense than she had ever experienced.

"Nikki?" Quinn's voice carried through the now thin layer of snow. "Nikki, are you in there?"

"We're here!" Nikki cried out as her mind spun with the realization that it was Quinn on the other side of the snow. "We're both here."

"Stay away from the opening, we're coming to get you." Quinn's voice trembled as he spoke.

Nikki wondered if it was the cold, or the relief of finding them.

"Back farther." Kyle guided her away from the entrance. "When they break through, more snow could slide."

"No more snow." Nikki gulped back a sob and a laugh at the same time. "Please, no more snow."

Seconds later the snow packed into the entrance finally shattered. A flashlight shone into the cave.

"Nikki?" Quinn's voice was clear now, followed by his presence as he peered into the cave.

"Quinn!" Nikki pulled away from Kyle and lunged towards him.

"Oh Nikki." Quinn sighed as he pulled her into his arms. "Nikki, Nikki, Nikki."

"No lectures, not now." Nikki rested her head against his shoulder.

"This is sweet and everything, but I'm freezing, in case you forgot?" Kyle rolled his eyes. "Can we save the heartfelt reunion for later?"

"Of course, sorry." Quinn pulled away from Nikki, smiled at Kyle, then led them both out of the cave. The trip back to the cabin was a blur for Nikki. She clung to Quinn's waist as he drove the snowmobile down the side of the mountain. As soon as they reached the cabin, Sonia burst through the door.

"Nikki! Kyle!" Sonia ran up to them.

"Sonia, you need a coat." Nikki climbed off the snowmobile. Coco bolted towards her as he escaped from Kyle's grasp.

"Oh Coco, my hero." Nikki crouched down and wrapped her arms around the dog. "I love you so much."

"I'm so glad you're both safe." Sonia hugged Nikki, then Kyle.

"So are we." Nikki's mother stepped out of the

cabin, followed by her father. "But you two have a lot of explaining to do."

"Yes, you do." Sonia smiled as she escorted everyone back inside. "Don't you ever take off like that without me."

"Quinn, it's Ken." Nikki handed him the box with the pictures and articles. "These should help with the investigation."

"He's already in custody." Quinn pulled her gloves from her hands. "Warm up in front of the fire. We'll talk it all through in a little while."

As the sounds of celebration surrounded her, Nikki felt the warmth of the flames, something she thought she might never get to experience again. Tears of relief slipped down her cheeks. Quinn sat down beside her. He wrapped an arm around her shoulders and kissed the top of her head.

"I can't believe you're here," Nikki whispered as she looked up at him.

"I can't believe you got yourself trapped in a cave by an avalanche." Quinn raised an eyebrow as he looked into her eyes. "But we'll have plenty of time to talk about that later."

"I don't ever want to talk about it. Ever." Nikki closed her eyes, then felt Coco's nose against her cheek. "Don't worry, buddy, I'm okay." She smiled as she pet the dog.

Christmas music began to play. She savored the warmth of Quinn's arm around her, the crackling of the fire, the sounds of the voices of the people that she loved, and the magic of the miraculous moment.

The End

WAGGING TAIL COZY MYSTERIES

Murder at Pawprint Creek (Prequel)

Murder at Pooch Park

Murder at the Pet Boutique

SAGE GARDENS COZY MYSTERIES

Birthdays Can Be Deadly

Money Can Be Deadly

Trust Can Be Deadly

Ties Can Be Deadly

Rocks Can Be Deadly

Jewelry Can Be Deadly

Numbers Can Be Deadly

Memories Can Be Deadly

Paintings Can Be Deadly

Snow Can Be Deadly

Tea Can Be Deadly

Greed Can Be Deadly

Clutter Can Be Deadly

CHOCOLATE CENTERED COZY MYSTERIES

The Sweet Smell of Murder

A Deadly Delicious Delivery

A Bitter Sweet Murder

A Treacherous Tasty Trail

Pastry and Peril

Trouble and Treats

Fudge Films and Felonies

Custom-Made Murder

Skydiving, Soufflés and Sabotage

Christmas Chocolates and Crimes

Hot Chocolate and Homicide

Chocolate Caramels and Conmen

Picnics, Pies and Lies

DUNE HOUSE COZY MYSTERIES

Seaside Secrets

Boats and Bad Guys

Treasured History

Hidden Hideaways

Dodgy Dealings

Suspects and Surprises

Ruffled Feathers

A Fishy Discovery

Danger in the Depths

Celebrities and Chaos

Pups, Pilots and Peril

Tides, Trails and Trouble

Racing and Robberies

Athletes and Alibis

DONUT TRUCK COZY MYSTERIES

Deadly Deals and Donuts

Fatal Festive Donuts

Bunny Donuts and a Body

BEKKI THE BEAUTICIAN COZY MYSTERIES

Hairspray and Homicide

A Dyed Blonde and a Dead Body

Mascara and Murder

Pageant and Poison

Conditioner and a Corpse

Mistletoe, Makeup and Murder

Hairpin, Hair Dryer and Homicide

Blush, a Bride and a Body

Shampoo and a Stiff

Cosmetics, a Cruise and a Killer

Lipstick, a Long Iron and Lifeless

Camping, Concealer and Criminals

Treated and Dyed

A Wrinkle-Free Murder

A MACARON PATISSERIE COZY MYSTERY
SERIES

Sifting for Suspects

Recipes and Revenge

Mansions, Macarons and Murder

NUTS ABOUT NUTS COZY MYSTERIES

A Tough Case to Crack

A Seed of Doubt

Roasted Penuts and Peril

HEAVENLY HIGHLAND INN COZY MYSTERIES

Murdering the Roses

Dead in the Daisies

Killing the Carnations

Drowning the Daffodils

Suffocating the Sunflowers

Books, Bullets and Blooms

A Deadly Serious Gardening Contest

A Bridal Bouquet and a Body

Digging for Dirt

WENDY THE WEDDING PLANNER COZY
MYSTERIES

Matrimony, Money and Murder

Chefs, Ceremonies and Crimes

Knives and Nuptials

Mice, Marriage and Murder

ABOUT THE AUTHOR

Cindy Bell is a USA Today and Wall Street Journal Bestselling Author. She is the author of the cozy mystery series Wagging Tail, Donut Truck, Dune House, Sage Gardens, Chocolate Centered, Macaron Patisserie, Nuts about Nuts, Bekki the Beautician, Heavenly Highland Inn and Wendy the Wedding Planner.

Cindy has always loved reading, but it is only recently that she has discovered her passion for writing romantic cozy mysteries. She loves walking along the beach thinking of the next adventure her characters can embark on.

You can sign up for her newsletter so you are notified of her latest releases at http://www.cindybellbooks.com.

Made in United States
Orlando, FL
19 December 2023

41144546R00124